ROMEO'S EX

ROMEO'S EX
·ROSALINE'S STORY·

Lisa Fiedler

HENRY HOLT AND COMPANY
NEW YORK

The author wishes to acknowledge, with much gratitude,
Mrs. Betsy Sorrentino and her 2003 freshman English class
for their comments and insights, especially Dug-Ho Jin,
who suggested Romeo's faulty memory.

Henry Holt and Company, LLC
Publishers since 1866
175 Fifth Avenue
New York, New York 10010
www.henryholtchildrensbooks.com

Henry Holt® is a registered trademark of Henry Holt and Company, LLC.
Copyright © 2006 by Lisa Fiedler
Distributed in Canada by H. B. Fenn and Company Ltd.

Library of Congress Cataloging-in-Publication Data
Fiedler, Lisa.
Romeo's ex : Rosaline's story / Lisa Fiedler.—1st ed.
p.   cm.
Summary: In a story based on the Shakespeare play, sixteen-year-old Rosaline, who is
studying to be a healer, becomes romantically entangled with the Montague family even as
her beloved young cousin, Juliet Capulet, defies the family feud to secretly marry Romeo.
ISBN-13: 978-0-8050-7500-7 / ISBN-10: 0-8050-7500-3
[1. Vendetta—Fiction. 2. Love—Fiction. 3. Healers—Fiction.] I. Title: Rosaline's story.
II. Shakespeare, William, 1564–1616. Romeo and Juliet. III. Title.
PZ7.F457Rom 2006   [Fic]—dc22   2005035692

First Edition—2006 / Designed by Jessica Sonkin
Printed in the United States of America on acid-free paper. ∞

1 3 5 7 9 10 8 6 4 2

For my Auntie Kiki
Who was, and is, like Rosaline,
"Rich in beauty." *
Grazie ... *for everything!*

And, as always, for my daughter, Shannon,
"... the hopeful lady of my earth." **

ROMEO'S EX

PART ONE

PROLOGUE

In a small cottage belonging to the Healer, Lady Rosaline did occupy herself with the business of tidying shelves and cupboards. With great care she arranged the multitude of jars and flagons containing herbal ointments and medicinal liquids.

The Healer was not presently about, having gone off near three hours past, with her satchel, to the home of an elderly man who had come screaming that his grandson's leg had been all but chewed off by a pair of wild dogs. Lady Rosaline did not doubt for a moment that her mentor would find some way to save, if not the child's limb, at least his life. No physician, nor surgeon-barber, nor dentist was more proficient in the art of healing.

Being alone in the Healer's cottage was not unusual for Rosaline. She had been visiting the place since her childhood and had learned much from the wise and gentle woman. There were those who feared the Healer, called her "charlatan," and "witch," but Rosaline understood that the people who shunned her friend were simply ignorant.

For years, the Healer had been her teacher. The old woman felt blessed to share her knowledge with a pupil so intelligent and insightful as Rosaline. More than anything on God's green earth did Lady Rosaline wish to learn the miraculous ways of the healing arts. Indeed, she prayed daily to the Almighty in heaven to grant her the intellect and the tenacity to see it through.

Now Rosaline opened a small jar and sniffed the greasy salve within it—the potent scent stung her blue eyes. "For burns," she said aloud, as though testing herself. "Also useful in treating resistant rashes"—she smiled to herself—"and protecting one's roses from aphids." She replaced the jar and was reaching for another when of a sudden there came an urgent banging upon the door.

"Ho, is anyone within? I beg thee, help us!"

Rosaline rushed to the door and flung it open wide. There on the doorstep stood a handsome young man; he was lit by the soft glow of a torch secured in an iron sconce on the cottage's outer wall. Rosaline knew at once who this gentleman was. He was about her own age, sixteen years. She had seen him before, from a safe distance, of course. Odd, this close he did not look to be the monster about whom she had so long been warned. In fact, he was quite beauteous, e'en as he struggled to support the weight of his wounded companion.

The injured man was some years older and in a sorry state. Unable to stand on his own legs, he leaned heavily against the handsome one. His nose bled, and his left eye was swollen shut.

"Beaten?" asked Rosaline, stepping out into the pool of light cast by the torch.

The unharmed one did not answer her at once. Now that she was visible in the glow of the torchlight, he could only stare at her, somewhat stupidly.

"What hath happened?" she demanded, more loudly. "Was this man beaten?"

"Beaten, aye."

"What is his name?"

"He is Petruchio. Or just Trooch, to his fellows."

Rosaline quickly wound her arm around Petruchio's waist. Together, she and the gentleman dragged him into the cottage. Petruchio's left arm hung limply at an odd and fearsome angle.

"Are you the Healer?" the handsome lord asked as they hauled Petruchio toward a low table near the window and lifted him onto the wooden surface. "Marry, you are so young . . ."

Rosaline ignored him as she tore Petruchio's tunic to reveal his bare chest, already crimson and bruising to purple. The gentleman stepped backward to give her room as she began her careful examination, running her hands over Petruchio's torso, pressing ever so slightly here and there. He let out a low groan but remained motionless.

"Broken ribs—three, perhaps four," she pronounced, more to herself than the onlooker.

Now the arm. Rosaline moved fleetly to the other side of the table for a better look. The sight made her gasp! His shoulder had been dislodged from the socket.

"Hand me your dagger," she instructed Petruchio's friend.

The young man's eyebrows arched in horror. "Think you to cut it off, lady?"

Rosaline frowned at the idiocy of the question. "The dagger," she repeated, and her tone brooked no argument. He withdrew the knife and handed it to her.

Rosaline leaned over Petruchio. "My lord," she whispered, willing her voice to be sweet, calm. "My lord, I bid you open your mouth. Just a small bit."

Petruchio's eyes fluttered, his lips parted.

"Excellent, sir. Now, here is your friend's dagger. I would have you clamp your teeth round the handle—firmly, aye. Like that. Very good."

Rosaline closed her eyes and placed her hands gingerly upon the patient's shoulder. She applied only a whisper of pressure at first, prying as gently as she dared.

"Aaaagggghhh . . ."

"Bite down, sir. Bite down!"

Rosaline executed her next movement so quickly that the onlooker was not even sure she had acted at all until he heard the noise that followed. 'Twas a roar of profound agony that ripped from Petruchio's lungs as the lady deftly slammed the damaged joint back into its place.

And in the next heartbeat the noise changed to a low hum, a murmur of gratitude and relief. Petruchio opened his eyes and sought those of his savior; she gave him a serene smile. With his teeth still gripping the dagger, Petruchio smiled back.

Rosaline stood and collected several small bottles and a clean cloth. "Tell me," she said, addressing her patient's friend, "what villain is responsible for this man's condition? Should we summon the constable?"

The nobleman said, "I think not, lady. 'Twas the constable who did pummel Petruchio."

Rosaline froze, the cloth she would use to clean the abrasions poised above her patient's swollen cheek. "Be this man a criminal?"

"Nay. Poor Trooch here is merely an unfortunate rogue who was caught dallying with a comely wench. As it happens, the wench is the constable's wife."

Rosaline's mouth dropped open in disbelief. "Never say thus!"

The young man nodded. "The constable saw fit to punish him for his trespass, not with the letter of the law but with his meaty fists."

For nearly half an hour, Rosaline carefully purified the

wounds and applied the healing salves. Then she used long scraps of clean muslin to securely wrap his mid-section.

"'Tis the best I can do for his ribs," she explained. "They will heal in time."

The gentleman was gazing at her in a way Rosaline found most disconcerting. He said nothing, just stared. Rosaline turned her back to the man, whom she was beginning to suspect was a simpleton. "He should not be moved from here tonight." She began to clear away the bloody pieces of cloth. "Collect him on the morrow, after noon." She peered over her shoulder at Petruchio's friend. "Do you understand?"

"You are exquisitely beautiful."

Rosaline pursed her lips impatiently. "That, sir, is irrelevant."

"Not to me. To me it is most relevant."

Rosaline sighed. "Very well, then. I thank thee for the compliment. Now, you'd best depart so that Pooch . . ."

"Trooch."

"So that *Trooch* may rest." Rosaline gathered the jars of ointment and headed for the cupboard.

"Your name, lady?"

For a moment, Rosaline considered telling him the truth of it—that she was a Capulet. What smooth reply might he have to that? she wondered, smiling. But all she supplied was "I am Rosaline."

The man's eyes seemed to light at the sound of her name. "Magnificent. You shall be hearing from me, Lady Rosaline. You may depend upon it." With that, he turned and took three long strides to the door, where he turned back before stepping out into the warm spring night.

"And if thou art wondering," he said in a silky tone, "the name of the man who hath fallen in love with thee this night . . . it is Romeo. Romeo of the house of Montague."

But Rosaline already knew that.

ROSALINE

Such a season as this one Verona hath ne'er known.
It is the year of our Lord 1595, summer.

A fervent heat has settled upon the city, baking the
trodden dirt in the market square. I am comforted only
by my own whimsy: the belief that in such heat, all manner of magic is possible, for men cannot think straight,
and women dream chilly dreams. In the orchard, the
defeated fruit falls to the warm grass, and the smell of it
is lush and dangerous.

Equal to the heat is the hatred in which the city sim-
mers; 'tis a selfish conflict begun long before this summer. A feud so great that it has carved a chasm of anger,
like a moat, around the city of Verona. Beyond our
orchard-fringed borders, Italy is a country drenched in

the sweetness of painting and poetry. There are Venezia, Firenze, and countless mountain villages where goodness thrives and strangers embrace, calling one another brother and friend. But here in Verona, we greet our neighbors at sword point and demand to know *che casa?* What house?

Montague or Capulet?

Stranger still is the fact that the origin of this feud is long forgotten. What is known to all is this—two households, thought to be alike in dignity, behaving with no dignity at all. Montagues spit upon Capulets, and Capulets, in turn, hurl stones at Montagues. Violence begets violence, and each generation has been bred to carry the scars. The feud is our inheritance. We, who are thought to be noble, separate ourselves from the rest of the citizenry by the fire of our loathing, and the city at large suffers in its wake. It disgusts me, truly.

For I am half Capulet, by my mother's blood. Here in Verona, all of my Capulet ancestors have been born and died for centuries. (My father was born I know not where. Nor do I know where he now lives or if he lives.) So by birth this quarrel belongs to me. And if I must lay claim to it, I am determined to derive a measure of amusement from it. Such is the thought from which is born this morning's folly.

I tiptoe past my mother's chamber and slip into the pale dreamlike gloom of dawn. On a dare set forth by my elder cousin, Tybalt, I go forth to trespass upon lands believed unholy by our kind: Montagues' garden! For tonight our uncle Capulet shall throw a grand feast, and Tybalt has goaded me into pilfering the flowers which will adorn the banquet table.

I go now to meet our cousin Juliet—'tis her lord and father, my own mother's brother, who will host the evening's celebration. Juliet is my dearest friend, although she is younger by two summers. She is thirteen now and not nearly daring enough for my taste! For this reason, I have exacted from her a promise that she will join me this morning and sneak onto the lushly planted grounds of our enemy.

O, how bold! To decorate the Capulet tables with perfect blossoms stolen from the soil of our sworn foe!

'Tis an hour until sunrise. Around us, most of Verona slumbers. Juliet and I walk in the thickening heat of very early morn. But the heat is nothing compared to the excitement, for 'tis a most audacious errand we undertake at this shadowy hour.

Juliet is excited, but mostly afraid, unaccustomed as she is to doing anything e'en remotely improper. The smile she tips in my direction is filled with trepidation, but she struggles to summon her wit.

"How is it, dear Rosaline, that even in such heat, your hair remains unrumpled? Mine is already damp enough to wrinkle into angry ringlets."

Sighing, I bite back a smile and lift one shoulder in a

dainty gesture. "I apologize, if my perfection offends thee. 'Tis not my fault that I am flawless!"

To this quip, Juliet flutters her pretty lashes and presses her palms together in pretend prayer. "So true, cousin, so true! Mayhap thou wouldst at least attempt to humor me by breaking a sweat?"

Jules and I continue on our way, laughing as loudly as we dare. We do not wish to call the attention of our sleeping neighbors. As we walk, I roll the sleeves of my gown to my elbows, the soft linen creasing easily in the crook of my arm. Then I unlace the cording at the neckline of my dress—one firm tug and my shoulders are bared!

"Roz, that is scandalous!"

"No more scandalous than this mischief we are about," I remind her. "God's truth, it is so hot that I am a mere moment from removing my garters and hose! These clothes are more constricting than the rules we ladies must abide!" Playfully, I lift the hem of my skirt and tease, "Mayhap it shall become the fashion!"

"And mayhap the Capulets and Montagues will one day call a truce!"

"Neither seems likely," I admit, glancing at my shoulders, pale and delicate in the jewel-like half light. "But 'twould be nice, wouldn't it?"

"Which?"

"Both. Amity in Verona between the Montagues and Capulets, an occasion to be celebrated with nothing less than the ceremonial baring of maidens' wrists and shoulders!"

"How dost thou come up with such silliness?"

"I am merely wishful, Jules. The fighting, the hatred, it all tires me so. My honored mother was taught to hate all Montagues as hotly as does her brother, your lord and father. Of course, she is not the sort who hates outright. She cannot e'en bring herself to hate the husband who abandoned her. Still, e'en my gentle lady mother does regard with a wariness near to fear all who be aligned with the house of Montague."

"The Montagues," says Juliet. "A pox on them!"

She says so with such rancor that I must laugh. "You say thus, but know not why, other than that you have been taught it well."

"Aye, 'tis true." My cousin sighs.

"Bitterness hath been bred into your being, like that sable hair with its auburn streaks, those emerald-colored eyes so like your father's." I take her hand and squeeze it. "And just as you've been taught to be grateful for such beauteous gifts, you are told to cherish the hatred, to make it your own. But truly, what reason have you or I to hate a *name*? A lineage, a particular curve of the mouth, a tone of voice, a certain shade of skin, or shape of face? Especially since I know not what did first bring about the hostility."

" 'Tis a sound point to make," Juliet replies with a frown. "I have oft asked my Lord the cause of the quarrel, but on every occasion, he's swiftly changed the course of conversation. By the blood of all who have died in its wake, I swear I do not think he knows."

"And still you hate all Montagues?"

"I do, for I must. I am Capulet's daughter, whose legacy is hate. Often, I think I am nothing if not dutiful." Juliet sighs. "And often, I fear I am just nothing."

Before I can chide her for such thoughts, she asks, "What of you, Roz? Dost thou despise the Montagues?"

"I know only one of them personally," I admit. "And in truth, I find him quite bothersome."

"Because he is a Montague?"

"Because he is a pain in my backside. But in my heart, I understand that the same heat that blisters the brow of a Montague does coarsen the complexion of a Capulet. That is a lesson, is it not?"

Juliet considers this a moment. "What is the name of this bothersome Montague?" she inquires.

"Romeo."

We are nearing the farthest boundary of the Montagues' land, fringed with fig trees and long, lacy wildflowers mimicking the blue-tiled spires of the house in the distance.

The house of Montague, an edifice of stone and mortar and fury.

And the dwelling place of Romeo.

He is without question one of the handsomest men in Verona. He is energetic, clever, good-natured. But despite his undisputable goodness, he is most irritating.

And that is because good Romeo, heir to the fortune of the house of Montague, professes to be in love with me! Ridiculous, that, for Romeo does not e'en know me. My acquaintance he did make only one month ago. Ever since, he has taken to following me round Verona. He lies in wait for me in the market square, in the village, e'en outside the confessional at Saint Peter's, and accosts me with promises of undying love.

'Tis comical, of course. He does not realize that I am kin to Capulet. Were I to tell him so, he might rethink his supposed affection. Although it is just as likely this romantic boy may think it twice the thrill to be in love with his greatest enemy. How am I to know? What I do know is this: He smothers me with his fondness! I marvel that his teeth have not rotted from the sugared sweetness of his vows.

We arrive at the Montagues' border. I reach up and pluck a fat fig from a graceful branch. "The enemy's harvest," I remark, contemplating the fruit. "It looks most tasty." I roll the dark prize over in my palm.

Juliet eyes the fig with interest. "I have heard old Montague spends dearly to water his land. Clearly, 'tis a successful enterprise."

"By all means then, cousin, indulge!" I toss the fig; she makes an effortless catch, as though she is secretly dying to taste it. "You are as Eve in Eden," I tease. "Partaking of forbidden fruit!"

"I have never been this wicked," she whispers earnestly, pinching the fruit. A glistening smudge of its juicy flesh darkens her fingertips.

"Taste it!" I urge.

I sense my young cousin is struggling with a temptation far greater than figs. In the next moment, she has popped the thieved fruit into her mouth. She savors the plump sweetness.

"Good?"

Juliet nods. "This sweetness is unrivaled. 'Tis as though its sugar goes direct to my blood."

"That, cousin, is the taste of triumph."

With a grin, I take her hand, and we walk toward a most magnificent flower garden. Centered there is a grand marble fountain with a large oval pool. In the middle stands a statue of a slender nymph fashioned of pink-white marble veined with gray. Her hair flows in a solid cascade of shimmering stone, and her torso is wrapped in a tunic, carved with folds. A stream of water glistens like diamonds in the fading starlight as it pours from a tilted urn cradled in her arm.

I remove my small dagger from its soft leather sheath against my hip and with it begin to cut the heartiest blossoms that surround the fountain. Juliet, who is too cautious to carry a blade, pulls the plants up by their roots.

For a moment, I am so overwhelmed by the flowery

scents I do not hear the footsteps on the hard-baked earthen path.

"Roz!" whispers Juliet. "Someone approaches!"

"At this hour? Impossible."

But she is correct. I hear the sound of whistling coming from behind a tall privet hedge. Juliet gasps, dropping the broad handful of lilies she's collected. The whistling grows clearer. I grip the stalks of my flowers so that they bleed their cool nectar into my palm.

Juliet's eyes are round with terror. This playful prank has become suddenly a dangerous quest. There is no telling what sin a Montague guard might choose to deliver upon us.

"Hide!" I command. "Quickly."

Without a second thought, Juliet flings herself behind the fountain. I bend to retrieve her lilies then make to join her, but the toe of my slipper catches in the hem of my gown. I stumble, landing on my knees on the stone-scattered path. In the next moment, squinting across the shadowy distance, I see not a guard but Romeo himself, rounding the corner of the hedge. My only hope is that in the dimness, he will not know 'tis I. But Romeo, it seems, has committed my very outline to memory. He stops a moment, then hurries toward me. A more awkward circumstance I have ne'er known.

"Rosaline?" He smiles. "Ah, my sweet Rosaline!"

"I am no one's Rosaline but my own," I mutter, rising from the ground with as much dignity as I can muster. I consider righting my neckline but realize, from the way Romeo is staring, that it is already too late for modesty.

"I am as honored as I am stunned, dear lady," he says with a gallant bow, "to find thee here awaiting me."

"Awaiting you?" The humiliation is unspeakable. He believes I've come in search of him! "Nay, sir, I—"

"In truth, 'tis most satisfying to know that you have at last sought me out."

I hold up one hand to slow his approach. "Good Romeo, sir, you are quite mistaken."

He hears me not, but takes my hand and presses the knuckles to his lips. "'Tis the answer to my greatest prayer," he whispers. "After weeks of my pursuing you, you come now in search of me."

I gasp at his assumption. In fairness, though, I cannot fault him for thinking thus. What other reason could he imagine for my appearing uninvited in his garden?

He smiles. "Please do not turn bashful on me now!"

Such dancing eyes hath he, such lovely hair, and what a handsome smile. And yet, his assets work no magic upon me.

"Come, m'lady, there is a gardener's cottage behind that hedge. We can seclude ourselves there and—"

"How darest thou!" My words come out in a righteous shriek.

Romeo blinks, sincerely confused. "So you have not come here to dally with me in a garden shed?"

"Most assuredly not!"

He bows his head, ashamed. "Forgive me, love. 'Twas a most insolent supposition."

I let out a rush of breath, which flutters a tendril near my face. "As long as we are here," I decide aloud, "we may as well have a talk."

He grins now, and leans against the rim of the fountain. "Talk, aye. Let us talk on any topic you wish, for the sound of your voice to me is an intimate caress."

From the opposite side of the fountain, I hear Juliet giggle. Romeo glances over his shoulder, but I swiftly turn his attention back to me. "'Tis a conversation long overdue."

"Go on, dear one. I ache to hear the verdict. Dost thou want me?"

Only to go away, I think, but will my expression to remain soft. "I am sorry, my lord. I do not."

Again, he lowers his gaze. "I have disappointed thee somehow. I am unworthy."

His dejection is palpable, and despite my frustration, I wish to comfort him. "Do not blame thyself," I say. "'Tis not thou . . . 'tis I."

"'Tis not I, 'tis thou?" Romeo repeats, frowning his puzzlement.

A coughing sound from round the fountain cuts him off. Before he can investigate, I take his hand firmly in mine. 'Tis time he knew the truth. For e'en did I think Romeo right for me, I would still see fit to rebuff his advances. "I've no wish to be loved, sir, by any man. 'Tis purity I strive toward, chastity I choose."

He is at first without words, but of course that condition is fleeting. "You fear only what you do not know," speaks Romeo, a warm look in his eyes. "I promise thee, angelic one, that once you've tasted of my passion, you will only crave more of the same."

Clearly, the expanse of his ego blooms as mightily as his garden. I let out an unladylike snort, but he ignores it, continuing his rebuttal.

"Passion is far preferable to purity," he confides, "and to be chaste is naught compared to being cherished. Love me but once, fair Rosaline, and you will love me forever."

"Alas, good sir, I am forsworn to have none of thee."

"Having none of me would make a nun of thee."

" 'Tis one way to look at it," I concede.

"But I have given thee all the words of love I know."

"Words," I sigh. "So many and yet so few of consequence!"

Romeo is momentarily lost in contemplation. I glance backward o'er my shoulder to Juliet, who is crouched low in the grass. When she catches my eye, she feigns to stab a delicate finger into her mouth as though to gag.

I turn back quickly so as not to burst into laughter. Romeo, it appears, has reached some degree of comprehension.

"So what you are saying is that you do not find my nearness unappealing—'tis simply that you have chosen, instead of love, a life of chastity?"

I nod.

Romeo gives his head a doleful shake. "So if you shall not marry, what then? Will the most beauteous Rosaline join a sisterhood?" He reaches forth to touch my hair, then pulls back, perhaps afeared an avenging angel might swoop down to lop off his hand. "Mayhap 'tis blasphemy to say so, but to cloister such beauty as yours shall be a sin most unspeakable! Beauty to a nun is none too beautiful."

He offers this wordplay with a smile so charming I imagine most damsels would indeed be tempted by it.

"I beg of thee, Rosaline. Conceal not thy loveliness in the dimness of an abbey cell."

I would not last five minutes in an abbey, but of course, Romeo could not know that. And as it would not do to have this impetuous boy tell all of Verona that I will one day be known as Sister Rosaline, I explain.

"I have no plans to enter a convent, nor any manner of religious order. Think back, my lord, to the night we met. What service did I render to your fellow Petruchio?"

"You did patch him up," Romeo recalls. "Quite skillfully."

"Well, did you fancy that mere chance?"

The Montague shrugs. "I thought it fortunate for Petruchio that in the true Healer's absence we found awaiting us such a lovely lady to tend his wounds."

I draw a long breath to hold on to my patience. "The fact is that I have spent years engaging myself in the scientific study of medicine, the art of healing."

"Ah." Romeo strokes his chin. "Well. 'Tis nice for a girl to have a hobby."

On my oath, I could slap him. I grind my teeth. "This hobby, sir, shall be my life's work. 'Tis my belief that I will best serve this world by wholly and undividedly pursuing my study of this noble discipline."

In a gesture most dramatic, Romeo lifts his arms toward the east, where red ribbons of light have just begun to show themselves. "She throws me over for the love of medicine?" he wails, dropping to his knees. "Ah. So be it, then!" Gazing to the heavens he beseeches the unseen sun, "Sinister star in your fiery firmament, burn me, I beg of you. Blister my brow, scathe my skin, dry up the very blood in my veins to dust, for 'tis only by suffering such hellishness that I shall persuade this lady to give me her attention." He throws me a desperate look. "And if Apollo will not malign me from above, I shall take the earthly course and ingest a fatal poison. Or stab myself repeatedly, so that you will be compelled to come near to me, if only to stanch the bleeding." He rises, turning his melancholy eyes to mine. "If illness is what you require of me, lady, then beginning here and now I will be sick."

Truth be told, I've begun to feel a bit nauseated myself! I roll my eyes, and from behind the fountain, I hear Juliet groan.

"What is that noise?" he asks, casting his gaze to the fountain.

"Noise, sir?" I lift my unclothed shoulders, hoping to distract him. "I hear no noise."

"A groan, lady. Methinks I heard a groan. There. Beyond the marble statuary."

" 'Twas only the sound of the water," I tell him. "Bubbling in the fountain."

"No, 'twas a groan, most distinctly." Romeo's eyes flare. "Is it a man?"

"A man?"

"Have you come hither to discourage my courtship by claiming a chaste existence, while concealing your lover behind this cursed hunk of marble, to witness my humiliation?"

"No, sir. You insult me!"

"I shall insult *him*," he says, withdrawing his rapier, "with the point of my sword!"

"You are mistaken, Romeo," I tell him, breathless. "No one is there."

"I shall see for myself," he barks, sidestepping me, then hollers, "Show thyself, man!"

I reach for him, miss, and stagger. There is a splash, and of a sudden I find myself backside-first in the fountain pool! My legs dangle over the rounded rim. To keep from submerging completely, I reach upward to grasp for the nymph's bare shins.

At the sight of me, Romeo forgets his supposed rival; he merely stands and gapes.

Much as I hate to request his aid, I find myself unable

to remove myself from the fountain without it. "Assist me, please!" I entreat through gritted teeth.

Mutely, he sheathes his sword, then reaches into the fountain. I clasp his wrist, he tugs, and—Hell's teeth!—he topples backward, pulling me down with him. In the next moment, he is pinned to the ground beneath me. We are nose to nose, my gown's soaked skirts pressed against him!

A gasp comes from beyond the fountain.

Remembering his rage, Romeo rolls slightly, tilting me from his person. Depositing me into the grass with a thud, he springs to his feet. With one hand on the hilt of his sword, he stomps round to the far side of the fountain and halts.

I await Juliet's shriek of horror, but it does not come. Romeo holds a moment, then lowers his weapon. "My apologies, lady. You are true. There is no one here."

I breathe.

"It was vile of me to mistrust you, my love—"

"Call me not your love," I fume, rising from the ground. "For I am not nor shall I ever be your love! You worship my face and nothing more."

Romeo blinks, truly stung. "'Tis not true, lady," he tells me. "I much admire your figure as well."

I am aware that in my soaked gown, every curve I possess is evident. The heavy fabric clings to my torso, my bottom, and my legs. I clamp my teeth tightly, to keep from screaming.

"Leave me!"

"Leave you?"

"Please. Now."

"But . . ." Romeo glances around the place. "We are in *my* garden."

"I am conscious of that fact, my lord. But I very much require your absence, and quickly." I indicate the muddy smudges upon my skirt where my knees rubbed in the dirt. "I wish to return to the fountain in order that I might rinse the dirt from my gown, and I fear that in so doing I may inadvertently reveal an ankle."

Silly, that, as my throat and shoulders have been bared since the onset of this meeting. But at present, I can think of no other way to rid myself of Romeo.

He begins to back away, gazing upon my countenance. "I shall not give up, dear Rosaline. My love for thee shall never cease." He bends to gather my scattered flowers to take away with him.

Juliet emits another groan, this time from beneath a leafy grape arbor to the left of the fountain. But Romeo has turned the corner and does not hear.

"He is gone," I report.

Juliet crawls out from behind the thicket of grape vines. Her lips carry an indigo tint; there are similar smudges on her fingertips.

"More forbidden fruit, cousin?" I tease.

"Aye, but Montague's grapes aren't near as sweet as his words. God's truth, the boy is pitiful." Juliet sucks the knuckle of her thumb, savoring the remains of grape flesh. "Doth he dream that any female would fall for such frivolity?"

"'Twould appear that he does," I reply, brushing at the mud on my skirt.

Juliet is thoughtful. "I imagine that when love is true, an entire volume could not contain the scope of it, and that the greatest of love is conveyed in a single glance, the smallest touch. Wordless love is love most expressive. A prayer unspoken. A wish one dares not utter."

For a moment, I but stare at her. Such poetic wisdom from one so untaught.

"I fear Romeo is more in love with love than anything," I remark, taking the blackish grape she offers. It bursts against my tongue and teeth, filling my mouth with its flavor. "But didst thou see him? He is fine to look upon."

"The statue did block my view," says Juliet, "so I saw naught but the bare backside of a nymph." She sighs. "Odd, but I am told to hate a boy on whom I've never cast a glance, and who hath never set eyes on me."

Taking in Juliet's slightly tilted eyes, her plump, pretty mouth, and her elegant bearing, 'tis doubtful their hatred would last long should they ever encounter one another face-to-face.

"Let us be gone from here."

Juliet is disappointed. "Without our flowers?"

Her lilies bob in the fountain pool where I dropped

them. I smirk, pretending to mistake her. "Dear friend! I myself am as possessed of my flower as ever I was before, although young Montague did determinedly endeavor to talk me into parting with it."

Juliet blinks at me, confused. In her innocence, she is slow to understand my wordplay. When she does, her cheeks flush near as purple as the grapes she has pilfered. "Oh, you are wicked, cousin!" She laughs now. "This corrupt humor from one who hath just sworn to live a life of chastity? Were I one to wager, cousin, I would surely bet against your succeeding at that goal!"

" 'Tis a wager you would lose," I tell her, gathering up my wet skirts as we hasten from the garden.

BENVOLIO

One more morning mourning among the sycamores west of the city where the leafy silence echoes the lonesome song of my soul. Oft do I come to this place, with turbulent thoughts to think. Thoughts I dare not share with even my dearest fellows, the rash and rugged Mercutio, who finds an icy edge of humor in all things, and good Romeo, my cousin and friend. Mercutio thinks not at all on the softer emotions, while Romeo thinks on them far too deeply.

In truth, until now I have been much the same as Mercutio. My doings with the fairer sex have been breathtaking and brief, magnificent and momentary. I promise nothing, and no female hath ever had the courage to require otherwise. I am told it is partly my eyes, which (to my disgust) are generally likened to a fawn's, and my smile, which I have heard these same ladies call crooked and disarming. Oh, I did learn quickly to use that smile to my best advantage, as a means to coax e'en the most demure maiden into bestowing her charms upon me.

Alas, this tactic hath become somewhat old. And empty.

Among the sycamores, I find the honesty to admit that of late my long-hidden heart seems as filled with longing as ever was the impetuous Romeo's.

God help me, I want to be in love. Would that I knew how.

I have tried, tried much, to fall into the state. And I have, on occasion, stumbled near to it, and soon thereafter tumbled . . . but a tumble is far removed from love. And as much as certain ladies wished to catch me falling, 'twas with scarcely a glance backward that I took my leave of them.

And still these ladies, when they greet me in the square, seem more than willing to allow me a second chance. Regrettably, there is not one among them that inspires me toward anything permanent. Mayhap if one of them, upon my cool exit, had demanded that I stay. But no. Every last one did lower her lovely eyes and allow me to leave. And so I did.

Long did I consider myself lucky to be so unbound by expectations.

But now such empty departures leave me wanting more.

Now in the distance, I sense movement, a gentle bowing of ferns and the rustle of low branches.

Someone comes.

I conceal myself behind the broad trunk of an ancient tree and look.

A man approaches. The pale glow of sunrise surrounds him, glinting off his hair. But e'en the breaking dawn cannot brighten this fellow's general aura of gloom.

No wonder. 'Tis Romeo.

Romeo here, in this veiled grove, accepting the morning as it spills in slanted ribbons of light upon the leaves, refracting the joy of it in his own despondent prism.

Romeo is sulking. Romeo is heartsick.

Romeo is nothing if not predictable.

In spite of my own troubled mind, I smile. Such a pair are we. Two youthful men in our prime, skulking about at sunrise, he all too willing to address his heartache, I compelled to deny mine exists. I believe he glimpses me in the periphery of his gaze. He does not call out, nor wave, nor even turn. Instead, he steals into shadow.

What is that he holds? A sheath of fresh-picked blossoms, though looking worse for wear. Lilies, their petals bent and torn. With a silent chuckle, I imagine how he's come to carry such a beaten bouquet. He holds it tightly to his breast, and I surmise that surely, earlier this morn, he saw fit to offer them to a lady who refused the tender token of his love. Knowing my good cousin as I do, I would not be surprised if he continues to clutch those stems until they rot within his grasp.

And with grim resignation I confess to myself that if only the right lady threw lilies back at me, I would likely do the same.

ROMEO

Chaste, sayeth she? Waste, say I!

What will medicine know of her perfection? A suffering man consumed with the horror of his illness shan't recognize the grace of her hands as they minister to him! Hands made to caress doomed to cleansing wounds, setting bones, bleeding the sickness from victims blinded by malady who will ne'er know nor care that 'tis a maid of most divine loveliness who heals them. Wherefore doth she wish to misuse her magnificence, to squander her splendor this way?

Rosaline is as this sad spray of lilies I embrace in her stead—the very ones she picked from my garden—listless now, and languid. Unloved they are, their beauty cast off, their legacy unrealized—and no buzzing insect shall ever carry away the powdery glory of such sweet scented blooms to live on in newborn buds.

'Tis clear Rosaline knows not what she shall be missing.

Nay, I will not quit my devotion nor abandon my pursuit. For I must truly love her to yearn for her as I do, mustn't I?

Aye, I must.

ROSALINE

By now, the sun has shown itself fully in the east. Another burning morning is upon us. Juliet, ever concerned for her parents' approval, hurries home.

I tarry in the square, taking in the sluggish bustle. Merchants and buyers argue over cost and quality; noblewomen worry o'er the wrinkles the warmth brings to their gowns. At the edge of the square is Saint Peter's, our gracious cathedral. From her steps, peasant children in dusty clothes call out to playfellows, darting hither and yon amid highborn strangers who would as soon trample them into the dirt. I pass a carter, whose cabbages are already wilting in the heat.

The air is thick with the aroma of commerce: I smell onions and garlic, newly cut wood, lamp oil, fresh bread, and fragile pastries laden with honeyed fruits. The world and everyone in it sweats, and the scent is primitive and divine. The lowly carry the musky smell of hard work, of honest labor, of hope, while the perfumes and powders of the gentry mingle in a way that is false and cowardly. They mop their damp faces as though ashamed of being human.

Tucked away from the main piazza is a small building of stone, liberally patched with earth and sod. A weathered shingle propped above the shuttered window bears a single word, shallowly carved: HEALER.

I rap on the sturdy door, listen for the latch to fall away. When the door pulls back on an ancient leather hinge, I enter the reassuring gloom I recognize so well.

She greets me with a smile. Her long hair is swept into a silver knot at the nape of her neck. Her skin, for one so aged, is smooth—the effect of a special cream she blends—and her eyes, startlingly clear, are a calming hue near violet.

"Good day, Lady Rosaline." She inclines her head. I do the same. 'Tis cooler inside the cottage than without 'neath the blazing sun. And there is no place I feel more useful, more at home. Indeed, my many experiences within the ramshackle walls of this hospice have inspired me to make the difficult choice I earlier described to Romeo. But my undivided pursuit of medical knowledge is only one reason I choose to keep free of amorous entanglements. For during these many months in which I have acted as the Healer's apprentice, I have seen with mine own eyes that for the "gentler sex," love is a most dangerous endeavor. In the course of our practice, the Healer and I have cared for those who have suffered greatly at the hands of their beloved.

I cannot count them, these women young and old who have arrived on this doorstep—some bruised and bleeding from having been beaten by their husbands, others fallen ill from pining o'er men who refuse to love them in return, their anguish so profound that many hath e'en begged us to administer some evil draught designed to end their very lives and thus their misery. I have observed too that e'en when true love runs smooth, the consequences to a woman can still be grave; for childbirth is a most unpredictable blessing, so suddenly can it shift from miracle to misfortune. Even the most cherished wife has lost her life in the course of an angry birthing.

And there are girls mine own age and younger, unwed, who come to us in mortal shame, asking if there is not a way to rid themselves of the growing babe inside them, a babe conceived in love that they would, under other circumstances, have gladly birthed and raised and loved. The Healer will not commit such surgery; she warns these frightened girls that it could leave them barren. If they persist, the Healer (with a reluctant heart) might send them off to the country physician who performs the act skillfully but in secret. Those who are lucky go on to marry and bear healthy babes. But many, lucky and unlucky alike, awaken in the dead of night, weeping for that one child they never knew.

That is the condition of women in love. And I refuse to join their tortured number.

Nay! All the poets, all the minstrels, all the Romeos on this earth could never persuade me to fall in love.

BENVOLIO

I arrive at the square to find two servants of the house of Capulet and a pair of mine kinsmen's own—a burly rogue called Abram and Romeo's boy, Balthasar—standing toe to toe. On my oath, I do tire of scenes such as this. Mayhap I should let them tussle and tear themselves to pieces in the name of this feud that is not even justly theirs. But nay, 'tis not in me to do so, and I know if they attack, I will be compelled to intercede.

Capulet's man, a long wiry fellow with little hair—I have heard him called Sampson—dares to bite his thumb at his rivals! (How bold he thinks himself to be, and yet how childish he appears, clutching his thumb in his mouth like a teething babe.) Montague's servants take great offense at such an insult, and in moments, swords are drawn. With a steady arm, I withdraw my own blade, and in three swift strides I reach them.

"Part, fools!" I command, commencing to beat down their weapons.

Balthasar knows me and stands down fast. Abram too sheaths his blade. I doubt the two dimwits in Capulet's employ recognize me; still, they seem to understand I carry some measure of authority, and they lower their swords.

I am about to remind them that the populace, not to mention Prince Escalus himself, has lost patience with the hostile mischief born of a feud 'twixt two stubborn families who call themselves noble (though I see naught that is noble in wounding one's neighbors in the streets). I am about to advise them to disperse. But I am interrupted by a firm hand gripped round my throat.

ROSALINE

My lesson with the Healer is disturbed by angry voices in the square.

Stepping out of the cottage I see my cousin Tybalt, removing his hand from the neck of an armed young man whom I know not. Even at this distance, I can hear their irate words, for the entire commons has gone eerily quiet around them.

Tybalt calls the stranger Benvolio and promptly threatens his life.

"I do but keep the peace," this Benvolio informs my kinsman.

I breathe, relieved at his assurance. Although he appears to be Tybalt's equal in all outward manner, 'tis clear that the one called Benvolio is not near as fiery as my catlike cousin, but he is every bit as proud. And handsome. I cannot help but admire his broad shoulders and the way those longish locks of rich mahogany-colored hair brush o'er them. In profile, he is splendid, squaring off with Tybalt.

But now, alas, as men so often do, this Benvolio doth contradict his own wisdom. *"Put up thy sword,"* he says in a hot voice. Tybalt does not hesitate to do so. Benvolio hastily amends his challenge, though not from fear, I can tell, rather, from a quick return of prudence: *"Or manage it to part these men with me."*

My cousin would sooner be drawn and quartered than abort a fight! His voice thunders across the silent square. *"What, drawn and talk of peace? I hate the word, as I hate hell, all Montagues, and thee."*

So Benvolio is a Montague. (This vexes me, though I cannot imagine why.)

"Have at thee, coward," Tybalt growls, his sword swooping in search of the peacemaker. Benvolio is fleet and dodges the blade.

Of a sudden, the citizens cease their silence. Enraged, they lend their voices to the quarrel, but they take neither the side of Capulet nor Montague. They holler out for peace, e'en as they attack.

Without warning, more of Verona's citizenry enter the square possessed of a deep, collective disgust, their anger surpassed only by their righteousness. They carry clubs and partisans, and cry out, *"Strike! Beat them down! Down with the Capulets! Down with the Montagues!"*

As I watch, appalled, from the Healer's doorway, my uncle Capulet and my aunt arrive in the market square. Soon come the lord and lady of the house of Montague as well, which ignites the turmoil tenfold.

My uncle shouts for his sword (his wife suggests a crutch!) and Montague, bellowing threats of his own, must be stayed by his lady wife.

'Tis nothing short of warfare in our fine common! Servants, peasants, the smithy, the cobbler, the cooper, farmers, and masons united in arms to rid their city of this selfish scourge. Swords clash in a sinister symphony; 'tis a steely skirmish, and my cousin Tybalt is as ever in the thick of it. His handsome cheek already bears a spattering of blood—his own or an enemy's, I cannot say.

I find myself searching the row for Benvolio, but my eye is caught by a shadow near a high gate, at the far corner of the square.

He is the one known as Mercutio, whose loyalty is with Montague. Frequently I have heard him calling out bawdy flatteries to passing maidens, and have even spied him on occasion when he believes no one about, using the dulled edge of a chunk of coal or calcite to scrawl wicked words upon the stony walls of town.

Perplexed am I to see him with his sword still in its

scabbard, apart from the fight. But even as the scrap worsens, Mercutio does not quit his casual leaning and merely watches the action. This strikes me as verily odd; Mercutio is known to be the most hot-blooded of the Montague camp.

He sees me seeing him, and for a moment, I wonder if he will smile. I expect he has a most dazzling grin. What passes between us is the knowledge that though we bear witness to the same scuffle 'tis with very different eyes.

I count off the seconds, convinced that in the next he will run madly into the melee. But when Mercutio moves, 'tis only to walk near the perimeter of the brawl; clearly he hath no intent to join it. He moves toward the cathedral, still looking for all the world as though he has no personal interest in the fight.

Viewing Mercutio's progress, I notice a small boy on the church steps, no more than four in years and shrieking wildly, though no one near him seems to hear, engrossed as they are in the battle. I cannot imagine how he's come to be left alone: Mayhap his cowardly nursemaid fled at the first sign of trouble, or worse, his lord and father has been pulled into the fray and now lies wounded.

Still shrieking, the tyke begins to make his way down the stairs to the main common. 'Tis as though he is blind to the battle before him. With his tiny arms outstretched, he sets to running . . . running into the heart of combat! 'Tis a gauntlet he runs, with swords swinging, fists flying.

As I watch, my heart pounding, I see him nearly trampled again and again.

Keeping my head low, I enter the ruckus. My eyes are on the boy and nothing else. Heaven save us, he has come to the place where the most violent altercation is occurring. 'Tis none other than Tybalt who stands above the child, dueling ferociously with some Montague (having earlier been jostled away from Benvolio by the human tide). Blades collide. One downward swing from either opponent will decapitate the child for sure!

Heart pounding, I shove roughly between two men pummeling one another and lunge for the boy, scooping him into the relative safety of my arms. His screeching is now directed into my ear, but I am still happy to have caught him. My only goal is to remove us both from this mayhem, and swiftly.

Keeping his ringlet-capped head close to my chest, I begin my retreat, ducking when I must, evading when I may, sprinting as would a hunted prey. Even so, I can sense that someone is watching me, though I do not halt my escape to see who. Mayhap if I had turned to determine such, I would have avoided the stunning blow which now meets me hard against the back of my skull.

The pain is like thunder, and I surmise, before the world goes watery, that I have caught the heavy hilt of a badly aimed sword. I stumble once but do not forfeit my grip on the child. I feel no blood—that is good—but the ache is fierce. A curtain of darkness closes across my vision but withdraws as quickly.

I am almost to the edge of the square.

Before me, a cruel peasant lad makes ready with his club to thrash an old man who has gone down on his knees to beg the ruffian for mercy. The attacker shows no sign of granting any.

Still reeling, I summon what remains of my resolve and manage to kick the young thug hard in the back of his thigh. The shock as much as the force sends him crumpling to the ground. He drops his club and looks up at me.

My mind swims with pain and terror, and I am surprised to hear myself blurting out an inane reprimand. "Respect thine elders!"

The erstwhile clubber gapes at me, then departs in a hurry.

I must be truly on the verge of death, for I believe I actually hear laughter coming from behind me.

Behind me . . .

I turn.

And the sky shifts, the world slants, I stagger . . . stumble . . .

But behind me there are arms, strong and sure, taking hold of me round my waist, lifting both me and the child I somehow have miraculously not yet dropped.

My eyes close of their own accord. I am no longer aware of any noise from the battle. 'Tis a mere whisper compared to the tumult within my skull. I carry the boy; my unknown savior carries me.

Soon the stalwart arms lower me to the hard ground beyond the battle, then carefully reach to relieve me of my precious bundle. Either the boy has ceased his shrieking, or the blow hath made me deaf. I want desperately to open my eyes but do not possess the strength required to achieve it.

A hand brushes against my cheek, then moves to my throat, pressing a thumb tenderly to the side of it to determine if any blood rhythm is evident. 'Tis precisely what I'd have done to a victim in my position. I can only hope the unseen stranger detects a pulse, for I myself am too far gone now to tell if I possess one.

Again, the hand—a soothing caress across my brow. Gentle fingers push aside my tangled hair, then return to my cheek, where they linger as the darkness comes to consume me.

BENVOLIO

I carry the girl to safety. She is not merely brave, she is beautiful as well.

'Tis with great care that I take the boy from her selfless embrace; even the child seems worried for her.

I touch her cheek, her throat (praise heaven, her pulse is strong), then allow myself the thrill of touching briefly her silken hair.

Would that she could open those eyes, so I might know their color and their depth! But the child is fearful, and I know she would wish me to remove him completely from the continued peril of this place.

I whisper a prayer that she will be well.

And another that I will see her again.

With a hopeful heart, I spirit the child away.

MERCUTIO

My good and gentle friend makes a most difficult choice. He leaves the lady to save the boy.

Oh, that is Benvolio through and through.

I, however, am not nearly so decent.

When heroic Benvolio is gone I approach the girl, who lies where he left her on the ground, hidden and a good distance from danger. I cannot help but wonder why Benvolio did not press his advantage. Why, he might easily have pushed her skirt up to admire her knees. He could have kissed her full on those plump, pink lips, perfectly parted now in what would surely be an invitation, were she not currently cataleptic.

Hell's blood, she is an angel, the sort to make a man's mouth water.

And she is brave. I saw her, as Benvolio did, risking her own skin to save that child. I imagine she is bright—not that it would signify, for a stupid girl can please a man just as readily as a smart one (perhaps more readily, for the less intelligent ones rarely think through the potential consequences of a careless romp).

She stirs, this beauty of unknown heritage. I crouch beside her, for I am curious as to what assumptions she will make upon her waking. Never let it be said that Mercutio declined a chance to dabble in some mischief.

Her eyes open slowly, and she looks much to me like a kitten. A sultry and desirous kitten to be sure. They are blue, those eyes, a shade near cobalt, and even in her hazy state, I see there is great intelligence behind them.

"Good day, my lady."

She blinks. I imagine lashes as lush as hers would feel exceedingly good fluttering against a man's face. Or elsewhere.

For a moment, she but stares at me. I have seen that manner of stare before. It means she is aware of who I am, and mindful of my reputation. She is likely thinking that while she may be away from the fight, she is not entirely unthreatened here in my company—for I present a danger of another sort.

"What happened?" she asks me at last. "Where is the child?"

"You were nearly killed," I state calmly. "As for the boy, he is safe." I have no intention of confessing that neither her rescue nor the boy's present safety is due to any effort by me. She continues to stare with those jewel-like eyes; I can almost see her mind working, wrongly surmising what hath transpired, how she arrived here, and how I have come to be hovering above her so protectively.

And now the angel smiles.

Were I not Mercutio, it might indeed remove me from my senses.

"Thank you, good sir," she says in a voice like a siren's song, "for seeing fit to rescue me."

I see no point in correcting her. Rather, I reply with a modest nod. She makes to rise to a sitting position, but I urge her not to.

"Rest, my lady. Any sudden movements will surely have you reeling."

This counsel, of course, pertains as much to myself as to her.

"You are Mercutio," she whispers.

"I am." I take her hand (soft it is, more so than any I have ever held before).

"I am in your debt, my lord."

She is, of course, in no way whatsoever obliged to my person, but why on God's earth would I ever dissuade her of such a conviction?

"If you say so, *cara mia.*"

"Rosaline," she breathes sweetly. "My name, 'tis Rosaline."

Beyond, in the square, there is a new commotion. I

turn to see that the prince has arrived. His Grace has long opposed this feud and is by no means an admirer of mine. Should he see me here, I know he would blame this day's dispute on me. Amusing, that, as it would be the first time I am not deserving of such reproach.

"Well now, my lady, I see you are no worse for wear, despite your courageous risk." ('Tis rare that I am compelled to speak truth to a lady, but that remark is indisputably valid; harsh incident notwithstanding, she is quite perfect to behold.) "Alas, I must take my leave of thee."

This Rosaline is full of surprises, to be certain, for she reaches up to touch my arm without so much as a blush upon her cheek. "When shall I see thee again, Mercutio?"

"I know not, fair Rosaline," I say, and that too is honest.

Were I inclined to love any woman, this Rosaline might just be the one.

But love is a dirty trick.

I make a quick bow and hastily depart. Her blue eyes bore into my back as I retreat. I can feel the icy heat of them. Helpless to resist, I turn once more and see them flutter closed again.

Rosaline. Valiant, exquisite Rosaline.

It occurs to me, as I round the cathedral tower and exit the square, that I may have just met the one and only person in Verona who could prove to be even more dangerous than I.

ROSALINE

The sun is bright against my eyelids, but I am wary
to open them, for I fear it may all turn out to be a
dream. Handsome is not the word for he who hath saved
me. He is beyond handsome. He is whatever compliment comes above it—beauteous, perhaps, or stunning.

He is Mercutio.

The pain in my head is eclipsed briefly by a new ache
near my heart as I watch him disappear round the side of
the cathedral. Were I not plagued with such maddening
dizziness, God's truth, I would chase him down. All of
me trembles; 'tis as though I have swallowed fireflies. Or
falcons. I recognize nothing of the girl I was just moments
before, the girl who imagined for herself a life of chaste
solitude. Aye, this me, this Rosaline, is altogether new,

for though I promised ne'er to allow myself the folly of romance, I find myself suddenly overwhelmed with a nameless longing I can only think is love.

Mercutio saved me. 'Tis more than reason enough to love him.

O, by the ecstasy of Saint Catherine, how is it I did ever think him crass? How could I, or any maid, mistrust one so heroic? I tamp down a curl of warning in my middle that reminds me this boy is a devil and a near Montague.

I have forsworn love. Denied it, insulted it, and feared it. Now I believe I am in it. I can only pray that Mercutio will join me there.

Rising on legs that shiver—as much from this remarkable realization as from my recent injury—I see the prince has entered the common. I would hear him reprimand the criminals, but the spinning in my skull is too alarming to ignore. I must return to the Healer's cottage and bid her see to it at once.

BENVOLIO

I find the child's nursemaid in the rectory, begging a drunken priest to assist her in locating the boy. A frail old woman she is, who became separated from her charge when the hubbub began. Her worry for the child is genuine, so I take a moment to calm her before rushing back to the scene of the brawl.

My wounded beauty, as expected, is gone.

But the prince has come. Prince Escalus, our noble liege, surrounded by his entourage of soldiers and advisers. I have much respect for our sovereign. He strongly opposes the feud but has until now dealt only gently with those who perpetuate it. From the look in his eyes as he glares at old Capulet and mine uncle Montague, I fear that the prince's patience has been tried to its limit.

I make my way through the now-subdued crowd to stand beside my kinsman, humbly prepared to accept the prince's wrath as deserved, for I too fought this day's battle. The monarch's words crackle with anger as he hands down his just sentence to the elders.

During the scolding, I reflect upon the girl, how she ran so boldly into the heat of the clash. I had watched her at first not because she was beautiful, but because she was brave. 'Twas only after I'd acknowledged her courage that I noticed her beauty, and dear God, what beauty it was! She had collected the child and was removing him from harm's way when the heavy hilt of a mishandled sword struck her. God's truth, I felt the blow upon my own skull. And still she found the strength and spirit to subdue a youthful hooligan before succumbing to the wound.

I am roused from my reflection by the commotion of the prince and the enemy taking their leave.

Now Montague turns to me and demands to know how this fresh brawl began. I explain 'twas initially the fault of Capulet's feisty servants, which is the truth, and that when I endeavored to end the discord, brazen Tybalt did react, taking out his wrath on my person. The townspeople saw fit to take up their own cause, that being when all hell, as they say, broke loose.

My account satisfies my uncle. His wife, however, has more personal concerns.

"*O, where is Romeo?*" she inquires of me. "*Saw you him today? Right glad I am he was not at this fray.*"

I find myself wishing my own good mother had lived long enough to worry after me on such occasions. Eager to calm the lady's nerves, I report that, indeed, I saw my cousin Romeo earlier this morn, in the sycamore grove. Of course, she is glad for his safety. So too is Montague. He reveals that lately good Romeo hath seemed troubled, possessed of a dark and cheerless outlook, which clings to him like weeds.

I am curious, as I had been in the woodsy grove. "*My noble uncle, do you know the cause?*"

"*I neither know nor can learn of him,*" he answers wearily.

'Tis said that speaking of the devil doth summon him. Sure enough, Romeo is suddenly visible lingering at the edge of the common in a shadowy gap betwixt a high wall and the constable's residence. He wanders as one lost from within, his eyes downcast, his steps heavy and slow as he trudges forth into the sunlit square to cast a long gray shadow of his own.

I suggest Montague take his leave. "*I'll know his grievance,*" I assure my anxious lord.

Lady Montague thanks me with a kiss upon my cheek, and again, as she hurries off, I feel a tug of loneliness for my mother. With a grateful press of my hand, my uncle, too, makes his exit.

"Good morrow, cousin," I call out.

Romeo lifts his head and offers me a sullen smile. Determined, I make my way across the blood-spattered common to meet him.

ROSALINE

The Healer prepares a tonic for my headache, and I drink it gratefully. She cautions me to forestall sleep until the dizziness subsides.

Stepping again into the square, I find I have missed the prince's lecture entirely. He has dismissed the perpetrators, and market trade has resumed. The carters' voices mingle in shouts as they hawk their wares.

The fishmonger cries, "*Pesci, pesci!*" The woman who spins exquisite silks sings out, "*Seta filata, seteria.*" Her handmade laces—*merletti*—are as precise and delicate as winter frost. Nearby, the handsome tanner shows his fine leather goods—*articoli di cuoio.* They are as soft and pliable as the tanner himself is rugged and strong. When they are not selling, he and the lace maker flirt openly with each other.

A farmer arranges his bushel baskets while his hefty wife boasts of the eggs she gathered at sunup. "*Uova fresche! Uova!*"

I glance round the square for Mercutio, but he has fled. I also wonder mildly what hath become of Benvolio. The crowd is thick; even were he still about, 'twould be near impossible to spot him amid this multitude.

Passing the gate where the cemetery path begins, I come upon Juliet's parents, my uncle Capulet, and his wife, my aunt.

"Good morning, Rosaline," says Capulet in his vigorous way. He is always so jovial. It causes me to wonder if he is hiding something.

I manage a curtsy. 'Tis unsteady at best, given the spinning in my head. "Good day to you both."

Juliet's mother gives me a look of strained patience, a tight smile. "Rosaline, you are bold as ever. Visiting the marketplace unchaperoned! Your cousin Juliet would quiver at the thought of it. She does not possess your taste for adventure."

"Mayhap one day it shall rub off on her," I suggest, suppressing a grin.

"Never say thus!" Lady Capulet exclaims.

Sayeth Capulet, "We shall see you and your mother, my dear sister, at this evening's feast, I trust?"

"Most assuredly, my lord. We would not miss it."

In the next moment, we are joined by a young man I know to be the Count Paris.

"Good morrow, sir," he says in his rich voice, then bows to me. "And to you, my lady."

"Paris!" Capulet beams. He claps the fellow heartily on the back. "Good Paris. How dost thou this day?"

Paris is tall and elegant, and many fine ladies would delight in securing his attention for their daughters. Paris is of the royal line, kinsman to the prince, and to my mind, he is duller than dirt. He and mine own cousin Tybalt were fast friends in their childhood, but 'tis no wonder they grew apart, for Paris is now as serious as Tybalt is wild, as cautious as Tybalt is brave.

The two men become engrossed in a discussion. I listen with only a corner of my consciousness, for the reckless spiral inside my head requires all of my attention. From what little I overhear of their conference, I surmise 'tis a business concern. It seems Paris is interested in obtaining some possession presently belonging to old Capulet, some item my uncle seems quite willing to trade, but not immediately. He recommends the transaction take place two summers hence. 'Tis always such with men; they think only of what they have and what they might attain, all for their own advancement. I see little point in tarrying here, so I excuse myself, blaming the pain in my head, and start for home.

I have ne'er before attempted walking whilst dizzy. 'Tis rather fun. For the ground seems slanted where normally 'tis not, and the road lies less than level, and the buildings to my left are suddenly at my right. I swirl without swirling, then weave and skip and arch to the sun. I leave the common far behind, the haggling voices of farmers and fishwives fading as the cobblestones trail off to grassy pathways dappled with wildflowers, leading to the outlying villages. 'Tis now well past noon, and the sun is raining fire, governing the day so everywhere unforgiving. My gown, soaked earlier from my spill in Montague's font, is dry now, and stiff.

Soon I come upon a servant of Capulet's, a doltish clown called Cardenio, gazing hopelessly at some dispatch; 'tis sure he is unable to read it. Were he any other of my uncle's staff I would happily help him, but this Cardenio is a snakelike fellow, whom Juliet once caught loitering near the open door of her chamber during her bath.

"Forgive me. You are Lady Rosaline, are you not?"

"I am. You know that well."

He smiles his reptilian smile and continues in a tone too smug for a servant.

"I also know that your name, which is Rosaline, is clearly writ here on this slip of foolscap I carry upon my very person."

"Dost thou, now?" I narrow my eyes in challenge. "Pray thee, sirrah, show to me which name is mine."

"Why, 'tis"—Cardenio's lip twitches—"'tis . . . this one." His knobby finger hovers o'er the leaf, then pokes at a name inscribed there. The name is Placentio. *Signior* Placentio.

"That is the name of a man," I say shortly.

He studies the leaf again, which I see is a list of guests to be welcome at Capulet's feast. Indeed, my name is writ there.

"Here," he says, tapping his thumb beside another name. "Surely these characters spell out the name of Rosaline. See how they roll and curve and link in a way most feminine? Surely these lovely letters can only signify my lady's name."

I snort at him. " 'Tis Tybalt's name to which you point."

Cardenio jerks his hand from the list as though it were on fire.

"Who read this list to thee? I know you are too incompetent to have done so on your own."

"True, 'twas read to me," he confesses. "And them that read it made special mention of your name." His chin comes up, his arrogance recovered. "Two nobles, lady, did decipher this language as a kindness to me. Nobles. Two of them." He sniffs importantly. "They spoke to me."

"And you spoke in turn to them?" I ask.

"Aye, and boasted that wealthy Capulet is my master who assigned to me this task—to trudge throughout Verona and locate each and all whose names are written here to inform them of the feast this night." His chest puffs proudly. "And for their service, I invited the two aristocrats to attend. Think on't. Two more learned, noble personages present shall there be, thanks to my own self. Lord Capulet will be twice further honored by their attendance."

"That remains to be seen." I frown. "You did not ask their names?"

Cardenio squirms under my accusing glare. "Would it be wrong if I had not?"

"Only if they be Montagues," I say lightly.

"Ah, well." He beams. "They did not say that they were, so surely they are not."

He is e'en more dimwitted than I thought. Without another word, I take my leave of him and amble on, praying the spinning in my head will cease before this evening's party. I turn my thoughts to the gown I shall don, what slippers, and which jewels. I will laugh with my cousins and eat fine delicacies. The candlelight will spark prisms in the crystal goblets, and Juliet will be shy and mannerly with the beaux who come to admire her. Several will beg a dance with me; I say thus without conceit or pride—'tis merely a fact proven again and again at occasions such as this. Having vowed never to fall in love, I have found such attention tedious indeed.

If only tonight the fiery-eyed Mercutio could be among that number, but alas, being of the house of Montague, he would ne'er be invited to a Capulet celebration. I walk on and lose myself in remembering the warm stroke of his voice. I go on in this manner for some while, until the sturdy wholesomeness of my surroundings thins, giving way to a section of town that is not near so inviting. My preoccupation with Mercutio, combined with the disorientation caused by my injury, has sent me heading opposite of home, and I have arrived in one of the most disreputable of Verona's neighborhoods. I have oft been warned by my mother to avoid this place and have gladly obeyed that directive. Until now.

I glance around, shuddering. The roadway is strewn with rotting food and other manner of waste I prefer not to identify. Mean-looking women wearing scanty garb lean lazily in doorways. An inebriated lout lolls in the filth of the street and calls out invitations to the harlots, who laugh raucously.

I am suddenly afraid.

The ancient buildings lean toward one another, forming narrow alleyways off the main road. The shadows of these forgotten lanes beckon coolly, but I dare not turn down one. I envision young ruffians, ensconced in these tunnel-like alleys, plotting awful things.

Dizzy, of a sudden, is no longer fun.

I find myself wishing for an escort, one strong and manly and fixed on protecting my person as well as my honor in this section of the city. I wish for Benvolio.

This thought stops me, midstep. *Benvolio?*

Nay, 'tis *Mercutio* I meant. Aye. The one with the dangerous smile. He who saved me.

Benvolio. 'Twas Benvolio who fought Tybalt. Whose hair

was a boyish tumble of dark curls, who sought to keep the peace, whose eyes, e'en from across the square, looked deeply kind and honest.

But 'tis Mercutio I meant to wish for. Aye, he is the rightest rogue for a setting such as this. 'Twas surely what remains of the dizziness that made me think Benvolio . . .

Heaven save me. Voices approach!

I feel the air lock in my chest. There are two voices, both masculine, drawing closer. The harlots take note and stand straighter in their doorways, puckering their painted lips in hopes of a day's wage. Panic fills me when I realize that in my disheveled state, these men might very well mistake *me* for a loose woman too.

For the second time this day, swift concealment is in order, and, praying no worse fate awaits me, I duck into the nearest alley. No sooner am I safe inside the shadow than the men come into view.

I blink, adjusting my eyes to the dimness, and see with utter astonishment that, again, 'tis none other than Romeo. And the one with whom he converses, I discover, is that tousle-haired, kind-eyed Benvolio, dusty still from the fight, but no less imposing. He carries a burlap sack slung over his shoulder.

I am far too relieved to wonder what business they have in this dirty district. My first thought is to reveal myself and humbly request their assistance. Forget that they are Montagues! In such a circumstance they could be henchmen of Beelzebub and I would not care. Romeo does not know me for a Capulet. Benvolio does not know me at all. To the best of their knowledge I am simply a lady unwittingly trespassing in the realm of degenerates and reprobates who might at any moment emerge to pillage me.

Benvolio and Romeo are deep in conversation. Just as I prepare to demonstrate my presence, I catch the drift of their discourse. . . .

The drift of their discourse is me!

"I say again," sighs Romeo, "as I said to thee in the square. The all-seeing sun ne'er saw one fairer than my Rosaline."

Benvolio's chuckle seems out of joint in this forsaken place. "And I, too, repeat mine earlier sentiment. Beauteous she may be, but there are others just as lovely, or lovelier. 'Tis only that you have not had occasion to compare. Aye, tonight we shall attend the enemy's ball, and in attendance there shall be a wealth of ladies, each with her own gifts to offer. And in seeing such an assortment of confections, my romantic cousin, thou wilt know that your Rosaline—for that matter, any lady passing fair—is merely one more delectable tart in a well-baked batch."

My fists are clenched, as are my teeth. How dare that rogue! To liken me, or any maiden, to *pastry!*

Romeo shakes his head in disgust. "I have already

agreed to attend the feast, but 'twill not be to challenge my taste for the sweet Rosaline."

"Aye, aye." Benvolio flashes a lopsided grin. "So you have said. You go only to clap eyes on Rosaline and . . . what was it thou spake? 'Rejoice in her splendor.' "

"Amen." With that, good Romeo takes his leave.

Benvolio shakes his head in Romeo's wake. "He is an impossible romantic," he remarks to himself.

"And you," I say, stepping forth from the alley, "are a contemptible cur!"

Startled by my ambush, Benvolio drops his sack and reaches for his sword.

"Go ahead," I challenge, my dizziness forgotten, my hands planted hard on my hips. "Slice me into pieces, as you would any 'delectable tart.' "

He stays his weapon. For a moment he can only blink in surprise.

" 'Tis you! The heroic maiden from the market square. You saved the child."

This remark has me waylaid—my stance softens, and I blush. "You saw?"

"I saw." His eyes fill with awe, respect.

For a moment I am touched by it. Then, remembering my anger, I arch one brow at him. " 'Twas hardly the act of a piece of pastry, was it?"

Benvolio blinks again. "I beg pardon, lady?" Of a sudden, a look of worry clouds his face. "You were hurt."

His apparent distress surprises me. "Art thou recovered? Pray, art thou well?"

Before I can answer, he catches my hand and brings my fingers to his lips. 'Tis a soft kiss he makes, a breath, really.

"I would know your name, my lady."

'Tis my turn to blink. "Hm?"

"Your name." His eyes meet mine. They are indeed as gentle as I had first believed. Darkly brown in color, with golden flecks. "Tell me your name, I beg of thee."

I have no intent to whisper, and yet I do. "You know my name."

He shrugs. "Nay. I do not."

'Tis a moment 'fore I realize he still cradles my fingers in his palm. I snatch them away, struggling to hold a thought. "But . . . just now, your companion spoke of—"

"Spoke of one called Rosaline, aye. 'Tis the only female he can think upon. He fancies himself in love with the maid. He has only just learned from her uncle's servant that she is a Capulet, and still he is not deterred. Says she is the most beauteous creature in all of Verona, nay, in all the world. Clearly, he hath never caught a glimpse of thee."

I am speechless.

Now something dawns upon him.

"Might I inquire as to what a well-bred lady such as thyself is doing here?" His wonder and concern are genuine.

"I am lost," I say truthfully.

"Praise be to heaven, then, for allowing me to find thee." He bends to retrieve the burlap sack, his eyes never leaving mine. "I shall see thee to safety."

"I would be grateful."

"Not near so grateful as I."

I fall into step beside him. Confused falls short of describing my condition now, and it has nothing to do with the blow to my head. Benvolio, just minutes before, taunted Romeo for being so romantic. And yet he kisses my hand and speaks in words as sweet as any Romeo ever hath spoken.

Sweeter, even. For Benvolio's ring true.

"Where dost thou lead me?" I ask, when I notice that we are not, in fact, leaving this cruel vicinity but rather traveling deeper into its heart. Odd, but I am not in the least mistrustful, merely curious.

"I've an errand to undertake," he replies.

We turn down a gloomy lane. An aged dog seeks refuge there in the shade. He emits a disheartened growl. Benvolio reaches into the sack and removes a leather flask. For a moment, I imagine he is going to offer me a sip of wine. But next from the sack comes a battered wooden bowl. Benvolio lowers himself to a crouch beside the languid mutt and places the bowl on the ground, murmuring softly all the while.

"Hot today, isn't it, boy? Smart dog, you are, Crab, to find thyself some shade."

"Crab?" I ask.

Benvolio grins. "Aye, that is what the residents call him."

I watch, my mouth a small circle of surprise, as Benvolio empties the contents of the pouch—'tis water—into the bowl.

"I told thee I'd be back, didn't I, Crab?" Benvolio gives the dog's ears a scratch. "Now, drink up."

The dog rises slowly on his feeble legs and begins to lap up the liquid. A contented rumble sounds in his throat. Somehow, he summons the energy to wag his scrawny tail.

"You are most welcome," Benvolio says to the dog. He slings the sack o'er his shoulder once more and begins walking.

"That was your errand?" I ask, hoping he does not notice the catch in my voice.

"A piece of it," he answers. "Come. I have one more visit to make."

Toward the end of the alley we come to a flight of dirt-and-stone steps, carved into the earth alongside an uninhabitable building, leading down, it would seem, into the very bowels of hell. Benvolio descends, and I, without a heartbeat's hesitation, follow him.

At the bottom is a cracked and splintered wooden door; Benvolio raps on it. A muffled commotion can be heard on the other side. Then the door swings open, and I am looking at what is perhaps the most beautiful—albeit the filthiest—little girl I have ever seen.

"Ben!" she cries, in a voice like music. "*Nonno,* 'tis Ben. . . ." She frowns over Benvolio's shoulder at me. "And . . . his wife?"

Benvolio laughs out loud, sweeping the child into his arms. "Ah, Vi. You know I have no wife."

"Aye." The girl beams. "Because you are waiting till I be old enough to marry!"

When she smiles, I judge her to be at least ten in years, for I see that most of her permanent teeth have come in. Those teeth are fine and straight, and her smile is glorious. Her hair, though long-unwashed, is thick and probably quite lovely when it is clean. It is pulled back from her cherubic face and tied with dirty string.

"By then, Viola," Benvolio says, placing her down again, "every gentleman in Italy will have already begged thee for thy hand." He feigns a pout. "Alas, I will surely be forgotten."

"Never!" She giggles.

Benvolio steps within the dwelling. One could hardly call it tidy, but 'tis evident great effort has been made to keep it clean. Another child, a boy, comes barreling toward us, calling, "Ben! Ben!" He too is dirty and beautiful.

Now he and Viola throw themselves at Benvolio's shins and cling to his legs like two enormous cockleburs as he tramps across the room. They cry out in delight, enjoying the ride.

"This fellow here," says Benvolio, ruffling the hair of one of his captors, "is Sebastian." He leans down toward the child and says in a loudish whisper, "Dost thou remember what I taught thee?"

Sebastian nods, releases himself from Benvolio's leg, and sweeps a deep bow in my direction.

"Good morrow, lady," he says, though his nose is verily stuffed so as to distort his pronunciation.

"Good day to you, kind sir," I say, inclining my head formally and trying desperately not to laugh. Benvolio's eyes are shining.

"And this princess who still dangles from my knee is Viola. They are *gemelli*. Twins."

Viola promptly sticks her tongue out at me.

Undaunted, I respond in kind.

The child's eyes go wide at first, then she breaks into a fit of giggles, leaves hold of Benvolio, and dashes back across the room to throw herself into my arms. Instinctively, I scoop her up and hug her tightly as she kisses me loudly on the cheek.

"I like you!" she declares.

"I like you too," I confess. I am struck by the resemblance she bears to Juliet when she was small.

"*Come si chiama?*"

My name; she asks my name. But surely I cannot say Rosaline, for then Benvolio will know me to be the one with whom Romeo believes himself smitten.

I am uncertain as to precisely why I prefer he not learn that truth just yet.

I am spared answering when Sebastian falls into a fit

of severe coughing. I put Viola down, go to him, and pat his back firmly but gently. He is so thin that I can feel the wet rattle of an infection right through his rib cage. Benvolio looks concerned but resigned, as does Viola. From this I understand that Sebastian's convulsive hacking is a sound not unfamiliar.

When at last the coughing tempest subsides, Sebastian snatches the bag from Benvolio. Viola lets out a shriek and pounces upon him, so that the two of them are rolling over each other on the floor—Viola attempting to wrench free the burlap sack, Sebastian clutching it with all his meager strength.

"Children!" comes a deep voice from across the room. "*Basta!* Enough!"

At once the children cease their antics; they scramble to their feet. I turn to see an elderly man in the far corner. I did not notice him before in the dimness. He steps, with a pronounced limp, into what little light reaches the burrowlike dwelling.

Benvolio bows his head respectfully. "*Buongiorno, signior.*"

"*Buongiorno*, Benvolio." The man turns to the children, who look properly contrite. "What have you to say to Benvolio?" he asks them.

"*Grazie*, Benvolio," says Viola.

"*Grazie*," Sebastion intones with a rasp.

"Now," says the old man, a smile tugging at his thin mouth, "you may claim your prize."

I wonder what that prize might be. Toys, perhaps? A

suit for Sebastian, and a gown for Viola? I find I am as anxious as the youngsters to discover the sack's contents.

Viola retrieves the bag, tugs it open.

'Tis . . . food.

Food.

And plenty of it. Bread—three fat, crusty loaves. And fruit. Vegetables of every sort, it seems, and a large wheel of cheese.

Viola is quick to tear a sizeable chunk from one of the bread loaves. She is about to have a bite when the old man clears his throat. At once, the pretty child crosses the room in my direction. God's truth, as she stands before me, I can hear her stomach growl with hunger. And yet she offers the bread to me.

"Thank you, no," I say o'er the thick lump of tears forming in my throat.

Viola glances at Benvolio; he shakes his head. Only now does she take a bite of the bread. Sebastian has helped himself to a generous-sized pear. I can't help but wonder where their parents are. I pray they are gone for the day to perform some chore. But e'en as I think it, I know 'tis not the case.

Back on the street, I again take in the desolation of the place. I no longer feel fear. Rather, I am consumed by the hopelessness of it all.

"So, lady," says Benvolio, a teasing lilt in his tone, "dost thou come here often?"

"Nay." I smile in spite of myself. "Though 'tis evident that you, sir, are something of a regular."

"I try," he says, serious now. "Their father was a good man. He worked many years in our stables but fell ill two winters past; his wife caught the fever from him. She passed only a week after he did. The grandfather does his best to care for the children, but he is old and without means."

We walk a good distance in silence. When we pass the women in their doorways, neither of us speaks, but I am certain he is thinking the very thing that I am—'twould be horrific if, one day in the future, Viola were found among their ranks.

Horrific. But likely.

I shudder. How is it that only an hour ago I could think of nothing but which costly gown I would wear to mine uncle's banquet?

At last we reach the safe boundary of the market square, though in far less time than I would have thought, or liked.

"I thank thee for escorting me, good Benvolio."

" 'Twas my privilege, lady." He crooks an inquisitive grin at me. "Lady?"

" 'Tis too bad that you will not be at the Capulet ball this eve," I stammer, to avoid supplying the answer to his inquiry. "I would like to see thee there."

His eyes darken. "You are to be a guest at the feast?"

I nod, as if in apology. "I am required to be. I am kin to Capulet."

Benvolio thinks on this a moment, then surprises me with his laughter. "It seems my cousin Romeo and I have e'en more in common than I knew."

I can only gulp at that.

"Tell me, why dost thou think I will not be at the ball?"

"Well, because thou art a Montague."

He waggles his eyebrows. "'Tis a masquerade, is it not?"

"Aye, it is."

"Well, then. What is the quandary? I can mingle with the guests—you, in particular—and no Capulet shall be the wiser."

"Brave of thee!" I declare, smiling.

"No more brave than you, m'lady. You ken that I am aligned with the Montagues, and still you speak to me freely."

I toss my head in a dismissive gesture. "To me, Montague is naught but a name. I have no fear of your friendship."

"My friendship?" His frown deepens. "So that is all you wish of me?"

I laugh. "Yes, that is all, and so you may relax. 'Tis known to me you have no use for love or marriage."

Again he looks confounded.

"I did overhear you earlier, talking to your friend, remember? You are scornful of love and other such silly sentiments. To be candid, I felt much the same myself until this day."

"Pray you, lady, what changed your mind?"

"Mercutio did." In truth, 'tis the first I've thought of Mercutio since finding myself lost.

"Mercutio," Benvolio mutters. "You are impressed with him, I take it?"

"Of course. He saved my life."

Benvolio's face twists with bewilderment. "*He* saved you?"

"During the brawl in the common," I clarify. "Just after I rescued the child. Did you not see that part of it?"

"No, I did not," he grumbles, then pauses. "And that is your only incentive to love him? Because he saved you?"

"He was there when I emerged from my stupor."

"Mercutio was."

"Aye." I can make no sense of the expression on his face. "I believed him to be your friend."

Benvolio grumbles a reply that sounds something akin to "so did I." His expression hardens. "I feel obliged to enlighten you, lady, as to Mercutio's viewpoint on the topic of affection. He is as firmly opposed to it as I." Benvolio lowers his voice to add in a mumble, "Mayhap more."

I step closer and touch his cheek. Bold, I know, but I will not deny that since this day's experience, there is something familiar between us. "You are sweet to worry for my heart. But please think no more on it. I will not be hurt by Mercutio. That is a promise."

"And how dost thou intend to avoid it?

"How else? By making him fall madly in love with me."

Something explodes in his eyes. He reaches out and takes my hand, pressing it 'twixt both of his. "Mark me, fair one. Mercutio is the wickedest of scoundrels, a wastrel, a cad. I know it well, for I am his closest friend."

"And what might you say of him were he your enemy?" I ask.

"Do not mock me, please. I am sincere in this."

"Aye, 'tis clear you are. I shall be careful. I swear to it."

For a long moment Benvolio simply stares at me.

"Tonight, at the feast," he says at last, "I beseech you save a dance for me."

"I shall happily dance with you," I tell him. " 'Twill be a joy to dance with so good a friend."

With no further word, he turns and stomps away from me through the square.

BENVOLIO

I think on nothing but the girl. All the rest of this day, into the twilight, my mind is full of her.

As I ready myself for the feast in the enemy's hall, I imagine her delicate hand alighting within mine as we dance—*if* there be time to take to my legs afore I am caught by some Capulet who wishes to break them. Perhaps I will persuade the girl to leave the feast with me in a stealthy fashion so that I may have her company all to myself. I will find us a place beneath the swollen moon where I may gather her close and breathe her in and touch her hair and ask to kiss her, and if by some miracle she whispers, "Aye, Benvolio, kiss me, please," I will do so as softly as 'tis possible for a man to kiss. My first task, though, will be to learn the great secret that is her name.

My fellows arrive, calling for me without. I don my mask, a clever, gilded affair of thin plaster that scowls on my behalf with thin, crimson-painted lips.

On my path to the door, I pass my father sitting alone beside the unlit hearth, and I see in his eyes that he will pass this eve, as he hath passed many others, with missing my mother. I touch his slumped shoulder, startling him. When he sees me in the garish mask, he almost smiles.

"Art thou well, my lord?"

"Ah, I am fine," he lies. "Please do not worry after me, my son. Go on to your celebration. 'Tis a masquerade, I take it?"

I nod; the mask bumps my chin.

A glint of humor softens my father's eyes. "Enjoy thyself, but take good care. And shouldst thou expect to be returning home at an exceedingly late hour—"

"Aye, Father," I assure him. "I will send a messenger round to let thee know."

"To whose dwelling place dost thou go?"

I evade the question, not wishing to reveal my destination, as I am certain my lord would forbid me to go. Instead, I squeeze his shoulder.

"I will be most cautious, and polite," I promise.

"What a fine man you've grown into, Benvolio. Your lady mother would be proud."

I do not reply, fearing my voice would catch. "God ye good night, Father."

"Fare thee well."

I hurry to exit, joining my fellow maskers in the street. Their torch flames burn like warnings in the unsteady hands of five or six scalawags invited by Mercutio. They are already deep into their cups and reeking of ale. I press my lonesome father from my thoughts and greet Romeo with a solid punch to his arm.

"To Capulet's," he declares behind his bejeweled disguise.

"Aye, to Capulet's! And may God have mercy on our roguish souls!"

The night is a swirl of stars and darkness and warm breeze, and my memory of the nameless girl. What mask will she wear, I wonder? Mayhap a nymph's. Or a goddess's? Some celestial caricature, sewn with flowing silk for hair like moonbeams?

As our procession makes its way to Capulet's home, glum Romeo, as expected, waxes on about the burden of his unanswered affection for Rosaline.

Mercutio, in fine, angry spirits, teases our friend, and does so with bold, randy humor—some windy speech about the fairy's midwife, the mythical Queen Mab. He wreaks his poetry upon us, casting a wordy spell as he chants on and on so that even the night listens. "Dreams, and chariots. Cricket's bones. Elflocks, prayers, and ready maids. . . ."

I will give him this, the boy can talk!

Turning my attention away from Mercutio's theatric ranting, I find myself wanting harder than ever to cross

Capulet's threshold. I can see the house in the distance, glowing in the deep night. The music drifts from its windows, beckoning me, inviting me to hurry.

I whirl on Mercutio. *"This wind you talk of blows us from ourselves,"* I shout, more harshly than I mean to. *"Supper is done, and we shall come too late!"*

Mercutio growls at me, then chuckles and rolls his eyes. He snaps me a bow of acquiescence, then strides off in the direction of the feast.

But Romeo stays me, with a heavy hand upon my forearm. His voice goes soft. *"Some consequence yet hanging in the stars shall bitterly begin his fearful date with this night's revels. . . ."*

I do as Mercutio did. I roll my eyes and laugh aloud, tugging good Romeo toward the party, ignoring his next words. Methinks I hear him speak of *untimely death*, but I will not abide such dark prophecy. Not this night, not when I am so close to finding love.

"Strike, drum," I cry in a voice of hope, marching on after Mercutio.

Sighing heavily, Romeo falls into step beside me.

ROSALINE

I dress for the feast in my cousin's chamber.
Juliet sits before the looking glass as though she does
not recognize the face she sees there. I am elbow-deep in
her best blue brocade, which she hath always said goes
nicely with my eyes. I have convinced her to wear her yellow silk, for the neckline is flattering, and she insists I
wear her sapphire pendant.

"Wherefore art thou so quiet, cousin?" I ask, just as
her maid lifts the gown's heavy skirt up and over my head.
I disappear for a moment into the mass of midnight fabric and cannot hear Juliet's reply. The heavy dress falls
into place upon my person with a rustling *swish*. The narrow waistline dips low, and I especially like the sleeves,

which are slit from the wrist to the shoulder and laced with gold cording to match the golden rope that swags from hip to hip.

Juliet turns from the mirror and smiles. "Perfect," she announces.

"A little snug in the bodice perhaps," I admit, sucking in my breath to allow the maid to fasten the gown in back. I thank her for the loan of it. In turn, she thanks me for the slippers I have brought for her to wear. They are dyed-yellow kid to match her gown, and they are only the slightest bit too large for her.

"You have said little since my arrival."

"Aye." She props her elbow on the vanity table and drops her chin into her hand. "I have been mulling over something my mother imparted to me earlier."

"And what might that be?" I twirl, watching the blue skirts of her exquisite gown bell at my ankles. "That you are to curtsy and say *buona sera* to all of your guests, and that you are not to taste the wine should Tybalt offer you a sip?"

Juliet gives me a look, and I know she is remembering last Christmastide, when Tybalt dared us both to drain huge goblets of burgundy. Juliet had three small tastes and fell promptly asleep. I drank my portion and hers, and later Tybalt graciously held my hair back as I retched in the orchard. "Wine is the least of my concerns."

I cross to the vanity to retrieve the sapphire necklace,

which I fasten round my throat. Then I pick up my peacock-plumed mask by its ribboned stick and hold it before my face. It covers my forehead and cheekbones, and my eyes are clearly visible through the almond-shaped slits. I wonder if Benvolio is on his way. Mayhap he has already arrived (and is anonymously partaking of Capulet hospitality) . . . with Mercutio at his side!

"Well, with or without drink, Jules, when the gentlemen take to fawning o'er you, I suggest you fawn right back at them."

"What mean you?" Juliet cocks her head as she takes her own mask from the marble-topped bedside table. Then she understands. "You are advising me to flirt this night!"

"Aye, and heavily. Flirt with every lucky beau who falls within your line of vision. Dance with any boy who asks, and if the opportunity presents for you to be kissed, by all means, Juliet Capulet, get thyself kissed."

I turn away from the glass and smile at her blush. She quickly attempts to conceal it behind her mask, which is similar to mine except that hers is bordered not with feathers but rows of large pearls.

"Kisses are sins," she states. "You should know that, being as you are a fierce advocate of chastity! Did you not, this very morn, hotly denounce the state of love and all romantic actions associated with it?"

'Tis my turn to blush. "Ah. Well. As to that, I have recently undergone, as they say, a change of heart."

"A change of heart?"

"Oh, Jules, it happened just today. I have met someone!"

"Met someone?" Her mouth becomes a dainty O of wonder. "Tell me!"

I fall back upon her pillows, feeling suddenly girlish and light. "He is the most gallant, most brave, most handsome man in all of Verona."

"Am I acquainted with him?"

"'Tis very doubtful," I admit, biting my lip. She understands at once.

"Oh, Roz, *another* Montague? First Romeo, now . . . what is this one called?"

I hesitate. "Mercutio."

"You jest!"

"Nay.

"Mercutio!" Jules shakes her head.

"I am hoping he will come here tonight," I confide, "so I may tell him of my feelings."

"A Montague here? Now I have heard it all." She sighs. "Well, at least you picked him for yourself." She grins. "Like a fig. Forbidden fruit. Could that be the source of Mercutio's allure?"

"It could. But it is not." I narrow my eyes. "What dost thou mean by saying I have picked him for myself?"

"I mean that you chose him." Juliet's eyes turn serious. "I have learned tonight that Count Paris does request my hand and that my lord and lady would have me accept."

I open my mouth and stare at her.

Juliet grins. "Could it be I have finally found a way to render Rosaline speechless?"

"Paris?" I gasp at last. "Wishes to marry thee?"

"Aye. As I told my lady mother, that certain sacrament has, until this day, been an honor I have dreamed not of." She shrugs. "But then what else would I do besides marry?"

I drop to the bed in a puff of blue brocade, nothing short of stunned.

"But Paris? I did not even know you knew him!"

"I do not know him, other than by reputation," she says in her sensible way. "But 'tis not as though the practice is uncommon. Girls are married off to strangers every day. At least I have clapped eyes on Paris."

"You have clapped eyes upon the village idiot, as well," I remind her. "But no one expects you to marry him!"

"Paris is not an idiot," she says evenly.

I scowl, crossing my arms across the bodice of the gown. "So that is your measure for marrying a man?" I snap. "If he is not classified as a halfwit, then he is husband material?"

"He is a nobleman. Kin to the prince."

"That is his pedigree. What of his personality?"

"I suspect he has one."

"Aye, and it is very much lacking." I shake my head at her. "A nun's confession is less boring than Paris!"

Juliet looks only somewhat discouraged. "He is handsome," she states. "In fact, Mother spoke at length of his beauteous looks."

"Likely because that is all there is to speak of. Paris dazzles the eye, aye, until he opens his mouth! Marry him? Oh, Juliet. How could you?"

Juliet sighs. "How could I not?"

There, of course, is the meat of it. I take her hand. "I am sorry," I say softly. "I did not mean to scold you. They have commanded it, then? They've left you no choice but to marry him?"

"On the contrary, they have left it mostly to me. My lady mother asked, *'Can you like of Paris's love?'* I am to look him over this evening and decide if I am able to love him."

"Based upon what? The cut of his tunic? The color of his hair?"

"I shall look to like," says Juliet. "'Tis that simple."

I glower at her. "There is nothing simple in considering a man for a husband!"

"Husband," Juliet repeats with a slight shiver. "Oh, Roz, hath any word e'er sounded at once so goodly and so grave? Paris, seen from afar, is the very model of masculine worthiness. He would surely devote himself in full to she who would become his wife."

"*Wife!*" I cry. "What dost thou know of being a wife? You are only just learning to be Juliet."

"Aye, and in so learning I have learned that to deny all

that is Juliet is what Juliet is most. Juliet *listens*. She *obeys*, and she smiles and thinks only what she is allowed to think . . . unless I am in your company, Rosaline, for then I am free to be some other Juliet, one who ingests figs that were ne'er intended for her to taste." She shrugs. "Whoever Juliet is, 'tis possible that she—I—will please Paris. Of course, 'tis also possible my ways will enrage him. Or confuse him. Mayhap he will laugh at me."

Juliet speaks as calmly as though she is telling me she believes it will rain. I spring up from the bed and commence to pace.

"And were he to laugh—at you, with you—pray, what sound would it have? A gusty, easy noise? A raspy bark? Heartfelt or forced? Could there come a day when Paris's laughter might be a joy to you, a thing you long to hear? Is his touch tender? Are his eyes gentle? What dreams did he dream when he was a child and does he prefer the heat of summer to winter's chill? Can he carry a tune? Does he favor his left hand or his right when he fences or holds his cup of wine, and how many babes will he wish you to bear for him? Is he forgiving by nature? Generous? Given to dark moods? Can he eat strawberries without swelling?" I turn to Juliet and throw my arms wide. "They ask, 'Can you like of Paris's love?' How in the name of all God's saints are you to determine that in a glance?"

"I know not." Juliet squirms 'neath my demanding gaze, then narrows a glare of her own at me. "Mayhap the same way in which you, this very day, determined you could like Mercutio."

She doth make good sense with that barb, and I look away, embarrassed.

"I know only that 'tis my duty as a daughter to consider it," she continues. "For as I have been honor-bound to hate whom they hate, now I must try to love he whom they find deserving of my love."

"And when are you to shackle yourself to this stranger?" I inquire. "This very evening? Before the ale barrels have been tapped, or will it be a long betrothal, lasting until after the honeyed cakes have been served?"

"Two summers hence."

I freeze where I stand. So this was the matter my uncle discussed so indifferently with Paris this morn. His daughter's future. Her very life.

"You will do what your parents ask?"

Juliet lifts her chin slightly. "Nothing more. And nothing less. *I'll look to like, if looking liking move. Whate'er truly means Juliet, mayhap this night I'll chance to prove.*"

Now Juliet's nurse, Angelica, hollers for us to join the feast. We exchange a glance that is part panic and part glee as we rush from the room.

The great hall smells of slow-melting beeswax and heavy perfumes, roasted doves and sauces of cheese and parsley. Wine and ale and apricots. The minstrels on their *mandolinos* wear puffy velvet hats embellished with ostrich feathers, and the guests seem golden in the gracious glow of glittering chandeliers.

Juliet and I watch a moment from the stairs. Tybalt appears and begins to taunt us. He is dressed, as always, to perfection, in dark hose of the softest knit and a purple satin coat, finely tailored. His rugged chin is scraped smooth, and his hair, the same raven shade as Juliet's, falls perfectly behind his ears to swing o'er his shoulders at a fashionable length.

"Why, if it isn't Ros-malign and Ghoul-iet!" he barks playfully, giving Jules's braid a tug. "Those masks become you, brats! For they conceal your hideous faces."

Juliet smiles and slams her yellow-slippered foot down hard upon his toe. He yelps, but behind his plaster mask his eyes twinkle.

"I shall take thee over my knee, urchin," he threatens.

"Thou wouldst have to catch me first," Juliet replies.

"Was that you I spied dancing with yon maiden, Tybalt?" I tease, nodding at a mean-spirited girl called Dorothea. She is exceedingly plump with dull, frizzled hair and thin, frowning lips. "Why, she's far prettier than your last paramour. Only, when you partake of her kisses, how dost thou manage to get thine arms around her girth?"

Tybalt sneers. "Dorothea is a maiden who requires two sacks," he reports.

"Two sacks?" Juliet repeats. "What mean you?"

"I mean," says Tybalt, "that were a man to escort her in public, he would needs bring along two sacks—one to place o'er her face and a second to hide his own, in the event that hers gets torn!"

Juliet cannot help but giggle at his icy wit.

"Tybalt!" I scold, slapping his arm. "You are wicked."

"'Twas you who pointed her out, Roz." He grows suddenly serious toward me in that way that older cousins have. "A lady blessed with beauty such as yours should ne'er mock one less fortunate."

He is right, of course, and I feel a rush of guilt. At times I believe that, for all his sauciness, there is kindness in Tybalt. I only wish that he would display it more readily—e'en to himself.

"O!" cries Juliet happily, noticing a recent arrival. "'Tis my old *spinetta* instructor. I must say *buona sera!*" She hurries off to do so.

Across the room, an elegant lady with a delicately curvaceous figure lifts her wine goblet to Tybalt.

"Now, there is a maid to my liking," he says, nudging his elbow into my side. "If I have not returned by Tuesday next"—he smiles—"be glad for me!"

He strides across the marble hall to claim his prize; I find myself free to search the crowd, praying that Benvolio has indeed come in costume and brought Mercutio along. Holding my feathered mask in place, I make my way round the room. Thinking unwelcome guests such as they would wisely keep to the shadows, I move toward the perimeter of the hall.

Let him be here, O, please let me find Mercutio . . .

"Benvolio!"

My new friend steps into my path, nearly causing me to collide with his broad chest.

"How is it thou knowst me," he asks, in a pleased but puzzled voice, "behind this mask?"

How, indeed? His visor is a full facade, covering his face completely from hairline to chin. And yet I recognized him immediately, for I sensed an aura that spoke Benvolio to me. Not to mention that luxurious, wavy mass of shining hair, and his sturdy shoulders. And a particular, manly aroma that is his alone—fresh air, strong soap, spearmint and cedar and clean warmth.

"Uh, 'twas . . . your boots," I fib, stammering. "Aye, your boots—there is a rather bad scuff near the ankle of the right one. I noticed it this afternoon.

Benvolio laughs behind his disguise. "She remembers my boots," he announces triumphantly to a fellow in a half mask who has just come up beside him.

"I would not be too proud of that," the masked newcomer slurs.

I expect my knees to waver—oddly, they do not. My pulse quickens, however, and I note a frantic fluttering sensation in my belly. "Mercutio!"

"None other." He sways slightly as he leans in close to me. "And, pray, what dost the lady recall of me?"

"Everything," I blurt. (That too is a fib, for 'twas actually his smug tone that gave him away. In truth, I did not know him until he spoke.) "Your eyes. Also your smile."

Mercutio chuckles. "'Tis better than boots, nay?"

I cannot see Benvolio's face, but methinks I see his shoulders stiffen, then slump. Surely he finds such love-sick prattle most disgusting.

I now spy another familiar figure across the room leaning forlornly against a wall and cannot stop myself from gasping his name. "Romeo."

"Seems she knows us all," Mercutio says, and I fear he means it as an insult.

Benvolio's spine goes rigid. "I will thank you not to tease the lady," he says in a level voice.

Mercutio snorts, plucks two goblets of burgundy from the tray of a passing servant, and hands one to Benvolio.

"To honor," he sneers, lifting the cup.

"To honor," echoes Benvolio.

"To honor!" Mercutio slants me a wicked grin. "*Get* on her and *stay* on her!"

Benvolio cringes at the crude toast. "Damn you," he mutters, ignoring his wine.

Mercutio yawns loudly. I fear he is growing bored and will take his leave of us, so I speak quickly.

"How dost thou, Mercutio?" I ask sweetly.

"I do well, lady," he replies, after a lusty sip of wine. His gaze creeps slowly o'er me. He takes another sip.

"My lady," Benvolio begins, "it occurs to me that I still do not know your name."

At this, Mercutio nearly chokes on his mouthful of drink. "By the blood of the devil, Benvolio! You know not who she is?" He laughs, his eyes steely. "O, this is rich, verily. Comic and tragic and sickening and delightful." He laughs again. "You wish to know her name! Marry, I have a notion—wherefore dos't thou not ask Romeo? I'd wager he will be able to tell you her name. He may e'en sing it for you!"

"I would be honored to learn her name by any means necessary," Benvolio replies, "but would much prefer she give it to me from her own sweet lips."

Before I can answer, Mercutio catches hold of Benvolio's chin and shakes it.

"She is Rosaline, you fool! Romeo's Rosaline! The goddess, the epitome of feminine perfection. The chaste one who has no use for him and yet causes him to weep and whine and waste away. She is *that* Rosaline! The one, the only!"

Benvolio freezes in his place; then, after a lengthy moment, he tips his mask so only I can see his face. "Rosaline?"

"Aye."

"Romeo's Rosaline?"

I frown. "Hardly."

"He is in love with you," Benvolio reports grimly.

"So I have heard."

Benvolio's eyes go dark. He looks at odds with himself, conflicted. Or perhaps just sad. "Why didst thou not tell me?" he queries.

"Because, if you'll recall, I had only just overheard you

callously assert to Romeo that I was surely no better than any other maiden in Verona."

"I was most incorrect," he whispers.

"O, Benvolio." Rashly, I take his hands in mine and squeeze them. "Please do not be angry. We had such a lovely time—"

"Lovely time," Mercutio snickers.

"And I feared you would want nothing to do with me had you known I was the cause of your cousin's heartache."

"Nonsense," drawls Mercutio. "Any man with eyes in his head would want badly to have something to do with thee!" He snorts again, rudely. "And I can tell thee just what that something is!"

Benvolio sends Mercutio a searing look, then turns and stomps away—I suspect to keep from killing him.

I remove my mask. My eyes sting and my heart aches, but I will not cry.

"Why, Mercutio, dost thou say such hateful things to me? You must know the depth of my feelings—"

"Deep feelings are of no interest to me, lady," he says curtly, taking another goblet from an attendant's tray. "However, should you wish to reveal to me certain other, more intimate 'depths' of your person—"

I believe I turn the color of the wine in his glass! "'Tis a most inappropriate thing to say!"

"Aye, and yet you are still standing here."

I find myself wanting to crumple to the marble floor.

Or slap him. 'Tis difficult to believe that he is the same gentle hero I met earlier this day.

"You have drunk too much wine," I surmise. "That is the reason for your boldness."

"The reason for my boldness is that I am bold," he says easily, downing the beverage in one gulp. "I thought 'twas what you liked about me. But then, what dost thou know of me, other than that this afternoon when you opened your pretty eyes I was near to thee?" He wipes his wine-stained lips with the back of his hand. "You interpret me badly, my lady."

"Then show me the truth of you," I challenge, stepping forward to brazenly place my palm against his chest.

He starts as though I've branded him with a hot iron.

"You play with flame, Rosaline," he warns in a thick voice.

"I shall take my chances, sir."

His eyes bore into mine. I wish I could say I see affection there. With a slow and measured breath, he grasps my wrist and roughly shoves my hand away, then whirls, a bit unsteadily given the extent of his intoxication. He takes two clumsy steps before turning back to glare at me once more.

"Wouldst thou join me, if I invited thee?" he asks with contempt.

"I would join thee, e'en if you didn't," I say, attempting a smile.

Something flickers in his eyes, and I imagine it might be regret. He turns again and lurches away down the shadowy hall. Despite the terror tumbling in my guts, I follow. But when I round the corner, I stop at the sound of voices. Voices I know well.

One is Juliet's. And he to whom she speaks is Romeo! Oh, this *cannot* be good! Juliet and Romeo . . .

. . . Romeo and Juliet.

They have concealed themselves in a curtained alcove near the chapel. The crimson velvet of the draperies shadows Juliet's pale gown with a bright, bloody hue. As I press myself to the wall and steal a look within, I see that she is removing her pearl-trimmed visor.

And Romeo doth remove his mask as well.

And I see them see each other for the very first time.

Silence explodes around them, and they gaze upon each other as angels might, angels who have ne'er seen another of their kind. God's truth, I can almost feel the heat that springs from them!

My first thought is to rush in, collar Juliet, and drag her as far away from here as 'tis possible to go. My second thought is this: So much for liking Paris.

Now they whisper something, and in the next moment, he has taken her chin upon his thumb and tilted up her face to his.

Hell's teeth! They *kiss!*

And whisper more.

And kiss *again*.

Oh, this is bad; this is *very* bad, indeed!

A hand upon my shoulder startles me. I whirl to find Benvolio. For a moment, I actually forget that nearby my cousin is kissing her sworn enemy.

"I believed you had departed," I say, smiling.

"I was about to, until I recollected that you promised me a dance."

"Then you are no longer angry with me?"

"I am many things with you, dear Rosaline," he says, "but angered is not one of them." He touches my cheek. "You offer me friendship, and I am honored to accept it."

"We shall dance then," I announce, deciding to leave Juliet to her own devices for the present. Romeo is not dangerous. He is just . . . nauseating.

Benvolio guides me to the dance floor and we take our place in the formation as the minstrels strike up.

The dance is formal and complicated, and twice I near lose Benvolio in the shifting circles. He is not the most graceful of men, but his persistence is to be commended. At one point, he is required to raise his arm in order that the lady to his left may skip beneath it to join her partner on the other side. But he is looking only at me and miscalculates, thus catching the unsuspecting lady with both his arms around her waist. He apologizes from behind the mask. The lady giggles, and I think perhaps she was not entirely unhappy to be wrapped, however briefly, in Benvolio's strong embrace.

When the dance has done, Benvolio and I take a seat upon the stairs and watch with amusement as the elders in attendance bicker o'er who, in their day, was the better dancer, heartier drinker, and most successful lover. And with no amusement whatsoever, we watch Tybalt skulking round the room, his hand upon his sword.

"Perhaps he knows there are Montagues present," I whisper to Benvolio.

"Aye, 'tis likely the case." He stands, pressing a kiss to my wrist. "Much as I hate to leave you, lady, I must remove Romeo from the gathering danger of this place."

"Wait!" I wring my hands. "Could you . . . might I . . ." Closing my eyes, I take a fortifying breath. "Will you tell me where later I might find Mercutio?"

Again that rigid spine and no reply.

"Never mind it, then," I say, forcing a smile. "I shall find him myself. I thank thee for your most delightful company this night. . . ."

Before I e'en finish the thought, he has turned and stalked away. I am finding that he does that often. I suppose if we are to be friends I will simply have to become used to it.

Glancing toward the chapel hall, I spot Juliet, who has at last seen fit to return to the feast—this due only to the fact that her stout nurse has captured her firmly by the arm and is all but dragging her along.

Romeo follows them several paces after. When Juliet scurries away to join her mother's table, I see him approach the nurse and ask a question. 'Tis clear he does not receive an answer to his liking, for his entire stance goes slack, as though he's been soundly socked, and e'en at this distance, I believe I see him tremble. The nurse goes to join Juliet, and I watch as Benvolio arrives at Romeo's side, urging their departure. As they make for the door, the nurse comes swooping back toward them. She inquires something of Romeo. He answers and exits quickly. Benvolio glances back at me and waves, then he too is gone.

Of a sudden, I feel inexplicably lonely.

As the hall empties of guests, my eyes dart round the room in search of Juliet. She is leaving with her nurse and looking utterly distraught. I surmise that her nurse has discovered Romeo's identity and has reported as much to Juliet. If she did not know him to be a Montague whilst she kissed him, she most certainly knows it now! With a hasty good night to those departing friends who call to me, I hurry up the stairs to meet Juliet in her room.

After the truth she's just been told, I am certain she will need me!

◆ ◆ ◆

I find Jules sobbing on the bed. Her gown is bunched into a yellow knot around her legs, and her hair is a cloud of darkness sprawled o'er the satin pillow cover.

"How did I not know it? When I heard him speak, 'twas the voice from the garden. Yet I refused to believe it could be Romeo."

I sit down beside her.

"Doff thy gown, cousin," I say softly. "You will surely ruin it, rumpling it this way."

"What care I for a silly gown?" she asks into the feathery pillow. "I would much prefer to doff my name."

I sigh. "The word *Capulet* is offensive to thee now, is it?"

"If it be offensive to sweet Romeo," she wails, "then aye, it is repulsive to me as well." She sits up, pushing aside her tousled locks so I might see her tear-stained face. "'Tis almost comical, is it not?" she asks on a laugh that is near hysteria. "You and I, who, in all modesty, could likely have our choice of any men in Italy, doomed to love two Montagues."

I allow a small smile. "I take this to mean that Paris is now out of the running."

"Do not tease me, cousin," she begs.

"Forgive me." I touch her cheek. "But, Jules, you do realize the Romeo for whom you weep tonight is the same Romeo at whom you laughed this morning? I will admit, he is handsome, but dost thou not remember those hopeless, hollow declarations of love he showered upon me?"

"He spoke quite differently to me," she whispers. "I felt the truth of it, Roz. Every word came from his heart with full honesty."

"How can you be certain?"

She shrugs, looking impossibly young. "I just am."

"O, Juliet. I do not wish to hurt you, but I must speak my mind to thee, whom I love like a sister." I fold my hands in my lap, praying for the harsh words to come gently. "Dost thou truly believe that the boy can be genuinely in love with thee, when just this very morning he professed to be eternally devoted to me?"

Her eyes narrow. "You are jealous!"

"Because of Romeo?"

"Aye, Roz, you are jealous. For all you spurned and scorned him, you are jealous that he has transferred his attentions to me!"

"No, Jules," I assure her. "I am merely wary. He loves me when the sun is up and adores thee after moonrise. He is too fickle by half!"

"Is it not possible," she says pointedly, meeting my gaze, "that he's merely experienced a change of heart?"

My words. She uses them against me, and I cannot help but think she makes a worthy point. Just this morn I believed myself immune to love, and now . . .

Again, she drops face first into the pillow and cries. Absently, I rub her arm, thinking long and hard before I speak again.

"If 'tis Romeo you love, then I shall do all in my

power to help you have him." Before she can react, I add, "But know you this, cousin. I am deeply worried for this match. You are both so very young, and unknown to one another. One kiss, for all the magic it carries, is little to go on. As I warned thee earlier with regard to Paris—"

"Who?" she asks from the depths of her pillow.

"My point precisely," I mutter, then sigh. "I ask only that you move slowly, Jules. Take the time to know Romeo and allow him the privilege of getting to know thee in return. Will you promise?"

She turns to me sharply. "I shall, if you agree to follow the same course with Mercutio."

I laugh. "Tybalt is right, you are an urchin!"

"An urchin in love," she croons with feigned drama.

I rise from the bed, removing the sapphire necklace and placing it on the night table before heading for the door that leads to her balcony.

"Should my mother send a servant round inquiring as to my whereabouts, have your nurse report that I am here with you, asleep, and shall spend the night."

I step out onto the balcony, which overlooks the orchard. Juliet follows me out there.

"What are you going to do?" she asks in a nervous tone. "Jump?"

"No, I am not going to jump." I hoist up the skirt of my gown and throw my leg o'er the side of the wall. "I am going to climb."

"Roz! You will break your neck for sure."

"No chance of that," I assure her. "Why, Tybalt taught me to scale this wall when I was but nine in years. We did it all the time. Did you not ever wonder how you came to awaken on the morning of your eighth birthday with half your hair cut short?"

She gasps. "You?"

"No, Tybalt. He was angry with thee for setting free his pet frog."

She plants her hands on her hips and glowers. "He told me my hair was sheared by minions of Satan as payment for the wicked beauty their dark lord had bestowed upon me!"

"And thou boughtest it?"

"I was but eight," she grumbles.

I hug her. "'Tis a most beautiful night. Why don't you remain here on the balcony awhile and enjoy it? Mayhap some stargazing will take your mind off Romeo."

"Perhaps I will."

"Where are you going?"

"I must speak to Mercutio."

Lowering myself over the side of the balcony, I find familiar footholds in the rough surface of the wall. The trick still comes easily to me, and soon I drop deftly into an adjacent tree. In moments, I am on the ground and running for the gate, into the street in search of Mercutio.

BENVOLIO

She is Rosaline, and Romeo loves her.

Alas, I love her as well, and mayhap more, but Romeo did spy her first. 'Twould be dishonorable to pursue her now. 'Twould be also pointless, for 'tis Mercutio she desires.

Unjust, that, and stupid, for he is unworthy. But the lady hath chosen—poorly, aye, but chosen nevertheless.

Fortunate, lucky, unworthy bastard!

The Capulets' house is empty now, but for those who dwell there. Romeo and I left some time ago, but I have since doubled back and loiter near the entrance to the grounds in the hope of seeing Rosaline when she makes her exit. Here in the street, the revelers disperse in high spirits, the jubilance of the night's festivities still clinging to them as they stagger homeward.

Now, in the periphery of mine eye, methinks I see the form of Romeo, running at full clip, toward the Capulets' orchard. So he hath returned as well, has he? No doubt he too hopes to spy fair Rosaline, who loves Mercutio.

Hah. We are both, Romeo and I, quite pathetic.

Now someone calls, "Benvolio? Is that you?"

I turn in the direction of the gravel-voice and find Mercutio, seated in the dirt, sprawled comfortably against the outside of the orchard wall.

"Come sit with me, friend," he slurs, "and share a drink. A flagon of wine stolen from the enemy's table."

With a heavy sigh, I join him and accept the bottle, which is nearly spent.

"Careful," he warns. " 'Tis mostly spit and backwash."

I toss the flagon; it shatters against a stone.

"Was that Romeo?" I ask. "I thought I saw him come this way."

Mercutio shoots me a sly look. "Mayhap he is avoiding thee, having seen you, his good friend and beloved cousin, dallying with his girl."

" 'Twas no dalliance, I assure thee," I grind out through my teeth.

"But not for want of trying, eh?" Mercutio laughs.

"We'd best both give up," I inform him coldly, "Romeo and I. 'Tis you she wants, though I have duly warned her of the peril inherent there. Still, she is determined to have thee at any cost."

"More's the pity," he grumbles. "She is far too good for me."

"Aye, she is."

"Too good for you too, Benvolio." He laughs again. "'Tis no secret that you are as shameless a womanizer as I. You, with your doe eyes and ready smile, would surely break her heart as thoroughly as I would."

"Do not count on it," I mumble. "'Tis a moot point, anyhow, for Romeo saw her first, and even if she wanted me, I could not betray him in that manner. We are friends, Rosaline and I."

Mercutio lets out a snort. I smile in spite of myself.

"You must be truly drunk, my friend, for you giggle like a girl."

Mercutio totters to his feet. "I am truly drunk but not nearly drunk enough. And so let us find that Romeo and go forth to increase my measly inebriation." He leans heavily upon my shoulder. "Call for him, wilt thou?"

"*Romeo!*" I holler. "*My cousin Romeo! Romeo!*"

We listen for his response and receive none but the sonorous echo of mine own shout.

Mercutio sighs. "*He is wise and, on my life, hath stol'n him home to bed.*"

I shake my head. "*He ran this way and leapt this orchard wall. Call, good Mercutio.*"

"Nay, I must conjure him." Again, he snorts. "*I conjure*

thee by Rosaline's bright eyes, by her high forehead, and her scarlet lip, by her fine foot, straight leg, and quivering thigh . . ."

I do not like the path his wit has taken.

"If he hear thee," I snarl, *"thou wilt anger him."*

Mercutio looks askance at me, for he knows that it is I who am angered by his bawdy talk of Rosaline. He releases me to stand wavering on his own.

I find that I no longer wish to find Romeo, for I fear I will see in his eyes a reflection of my own fragility. Suddenly, I am eager to get myself home, where I may pine in private. With a show of false humor, I clap Mercutio on the back. He stumbles.

"Come, he hath hid himself among these trees to be consorted with the humorous night. Blind is his love, and befits the dark." As does my own.

Mercutio agrees, and we begin our journey homeward. As we traverse the cobbled streets, I glance behind me once. Methinks I hear the sound of delicate footfall in pursuit of us. And the swish of a heavy gown?

'Tis impossible. I am only wishful.

ROSALINE

My exit from the orchard through a neglected and overgrown gate places me on the south road, and by some miracle, 'tis there that Mercutio and Benvolio have paused to call for Romeo. When he does not reveal himself, they quit the search and begin their trek homeward.

Keeping to the shadows of trees and dwellings, I follow them at a comfortable distance. There is a looseness in Mercutio's stride that tells me he is even drunker now than he had been at the feast.

They cross the vacant market square, and soon turn onto a street that winds gently upward. Odd that a rogue like Mercutio should live on such a quiet, homey lane as this. The walls of the buildings have been freshly whitewashed and seem to glow in the moonlight. Above, balconies hemmed with ironwork drip flowers and trailing vines. All but a few of the arched windows are dark. Finally Mercutio and Benvolio halt beside a broad doorway and bid one another a good night.

When the heavy door closes behind Mercutio, Benvolio hesitates as though he senses someone near. I hold my breath until he turns and continues on up the hill and I am alone on this pleasant *via*. The air goes blossom-sweet as a warm breeze troubles the mass of roses climbing the face of the house toward the upper terrace. A window on the second story suddenly blooms with golden candlelight.

The glow floats onward. A moment later, the balcony doors swing open, and the candlelight wafts softly into the night. Mercutio brings the taper onto the balcony and turns his face toward the silver circle of the moon.

He speaks. "Oh, Romeo . . ."

Romeo! He looks to the moon and whispers *Romeo?* My jaw goes slack with surprise, and no small amount of panic, until Mercutio speaks more.

"Romeo, wherefore art *thou* the fortunate man who first glimpsed and chose fair Rosaline?"

Panic turns to joy! 'Tis me he thinks upon fondly and Romeo he resents for claiming me first! I spring from the shadows to stand beneath the balcony and call out in a whisper, "Mercutio!"

He starts at the sound of my voice from below. "Who is there?"

I step into the pale puddle of light spilling from his candle. "'Tis Lady Rosaline," I announce as loudly as I dare.

He frowns. "How camest thou hither, tell me, and wherefore?"

"I came," I explain, stepping near to the rose trellis and taking hold, "by following you on your wobbly walk homeward." Testing the tenacity of the tall trellis with a tug, I plant one foot on the lowest crossbar and lift myself. "If thou canst not guess *why*, then thou art surely more intoxicated than I imagined."

I reach upward, grasping a vertical slat and hoisting myself higher, placing my foot securely upon a higher lath. The thorny vines snag the brocade of the gown, tearing at my palms and wrists.

"God's bodkin, girl!" Mercutio bends over the rail. "What in holy hell art thou attempting?"

I continue my ascent, easily scaling the leafy lattice, hand over hand, feeling for the safety of slats beneath my slippers. 'Tis no time before I have reached the balcony. Mercutio and I are face-to-face.

I smile. Mercutio does not.

"You climb this wall like an insect," he observes.

Of a sudden, I conjure a vision of myself as I must appear to him, clinging to the outer wall of his home upon this rose-festooned trellis. A most preposterous image, that.

I laugh. Mercutio does not.

"But then, a woman can be very much like a spider," he muses in an icy tone. "Spinning pretty webs in which to trap her victims. Didst thou imagine, Rosaline, that I would tumble o'er the side of this balcony in a lovesick haze to run off with thee into the night?"

In truth, I had hoped something of that very sort might occur, but his disdainful tone has me reluctant to admit it.

"Or dost thou intend to join me here in my bedchamber?" He laughs now. His breath reeks heavily of wine. "Oh, no, that cannot possibly be so, for thou art the *chaste* Rosaline." He narrows his eyes at me. "Or . . . art thou?"

Before I can summon a reply, he reaches forward to grasp my shoulders and pulls me closer to the rail. An unsettling cracking sound comes from somewhere near my ankles.

"Dost thou offer to lie with me, and didst thou lie to my friend Romeo when you told him you were pure and intended to remain thus?" His nose is touching mine. "Innocence is a curable disease, you know. Virtue, like honor, is merely an airy word. Mayhap your favors can be had for naught more than the cost of a promise?"

In the next breath, he has crushed his lips hard upon mine. 'Tis a severe kiss, a kiss filled with anger. I do not at all like it and am relieved when he releases me at last. His breaths come in shallow gasps. O'er the sound of them, I am vaguely aware of a noise like twigs snapping underfoot.

"Be gone, temptress," he grumbles. "For e'en if I had use for love, I would still needs keep my distance. Romeo saw thee first." For a moment, he but stares at me. His next words are colder still. "Away with thee!"

With that, he spins on his heel, enters the house, and slams the balcony doors behind him. I feel the force of their impact vibrate through the stone wall, and now, blending with the echo of the slamming door, comes the sound of splintering wood. The trellis gives way with a succession of loud cracks, separating from the wall, coming apart in jagged splinters. I fall backward, still clutching a handful of spent wood and thorny stems. I squeeze my eyes shut, and a shriek rises in my throat, for I expect to crash upon the cobblestones in a bloody heap.

But that is not to be. For I do not meet the ground.

Instead, I am caught.

Caught and cradled in an embrace both sturdy and sweet.

I need not open my eyes to see who the catcher is.

"It seems you are a lady who requires more than the usual share of rescuing."

Benvolio lowers my feet to the ground. When he is satisfied that I can stand on my own, he releases me and takes a step back. "I take it things did not go well up there on Mercutio's balcony?"

I shake my head, giving him a pinched little frown. "And if you dare to say 'I told thee so'—"

"Tossed you right over the rail, did he?"

"*Tossed* me? Of course he did not *toss*—"

'Tis not until I see his grin that I understand he is teasing. "No, sir," I say, smoothing my skirts. "He did not toss me. I jumped. I found I was unimpressed with Mercutio's sloppy style of kissing, and so I simply dove from his balcony to avoid more of the same. 'Twas a full somersault with a twist. Didst thou not see it?"

"I regret to say I did not. I was too intent on placing my person between your lovely body and these hard cobblestones."

"Aye." I nod with mock solemnity. "The landing has always been the part of the trick I most dislike."

He laughs, and I find I like the sound a good deal. "Come, Lady Rosaline, I shall see you home . . . again."

" 'Tis too warm to go home," I blurt out, surprised by how greatly I desire his company. "Might we . . . I do not know . . . might we seek out someplace cool?"

Benvolio studies me carefully for a long moment, then he takes my arm and we start down the hill. At the bottom of the street, he heads west.

We discuss the feast as we walk. He remarks that the port was of especially good quality. I tell him I did not have the opportunity to partake of any.

"I did, however, discover that your good friend Romeo and my—"

I stop in my tracks, interrupting my revelation regarding his cousin and mine when I see the place to which he has led me.

"The forest," I remark, rather stupidly.

"A grove, actually. I often meander here when I feel the need for solitude. 'Tis dense enough to provide concealment, yet not so dense that moonlight may not penetrate its leafy canopy."

He speaks true. Ribbons of moonglow unfurl from above, casting a shimmering blue radiance into the labyrinth of slender trunks and graceful limbs. I can smell the earthy coolness.

Benvolio indicates a narrow pathway; I duck beneath a low branch to enter the magic of the silent wood and follow the leaf-scattered trail. Together, we weave through streamers of silver light until we reach a fallen tree; by some chance it did land balanced across two large stones, forming a sort of rounded bench.

"Here is my customary spot," he says, lowering himself to sit gingerly upon the trunk. "Join me?"

Smiling, I do so. The trunk rocks ever so slightly as I settle upon it.

"Pray thee, lady," he says when I am seated, "may I inquire exactly what 'style' dost thou enjoy?"

I look at him quizzically.

"Of kissing," he clarifies. "Earlier you did mention that you were not particularly moved by Mercutio's style of kissing, and I merely wondered just precisely what style you are used to."

I do not open my mouth, for I know I will only stammer like a fool. What an unthinkably improper conversation! I find I cannot wait to hear more of it!

"To my mind," he goes on breezily, "I prefer soft, slow kisses."

"Soft, slow kisses?" I repeat haltingly.

"Yes. The softer the better. You know the sort."

Alas, I do not know. I lift one shoulder, a tiny shrug.

"I suppose you could say I like to linger when I kiss," he confesses.

"Linger?"

"Mmm, yes. Take my time, savor, enjoy. After all, what cause is there to rush a kiss?"

"None, I suppose," I reply in a whisper.

"Mercutio, I deduce, is not a lingerer?"

I shake my head, very slowly.

"A shame, that. There upon the balcony, with the enticing scent of roses, and the hot breeze through your hair, it would have been a fine setting for that sort of soft, slow kiss."

Soft and slow again. I believe I actually feel those words skimming o'er my skin. I remember back at the feast, when Romeo with saintly sweetness did bring his mouth to Juliet's, brushing her lips with his. And here is Benvolio beside me in this mystic grove, with only the sycamores to see. When did he put his arm about my waist? I wonder, though I have not thought to insist he remove it.

Soft and slow.

Linger . . .

Enjoy.

My face turns up to his, and a band of moonglow falls across his eyes.

You know the sort.

Alas . . .

Soft.

And slow.

"Show me?"

"Gladly."

Benvolio's hand at my waist presses me nearer to him, and I turn a bit, placing my hands tremulously upon his shoulders. He lowers his face to mine, closing his eyes. I lift my chin . . .

Alas, before our lips can meet, the tree trunk upon which we sit shimmies once, rolls, then tumbles off its rocky platform, spilling us with a muffled thud.

To the moss we topple backward, falling gently, head o'er heels.
Mayhap to land so safely on such softness is the way love truly feels.

ROMEO

Friar Laurence hath agreed to perform the blessed rites in which I shall take sweet Juliet for my wife.

True, the cleric was at first perplexed by my glad demeanor when I joined him so early this morn in his herb garden. He could see I'd had no sleep, but I told him I had no need of it.

"Wast thou with Rosaline?" he asked.

I assured him I had all but forgotten that name and the despair it inflicted. And I confessed to my confessor that I was now in love in earnest, a love whose very definition is the one who inspires it: *Juliet.* My adored adversary.

Aye, the friar did challenge my claim. He reminded me 'twas only one sunrise past that I wept for another.

But he is old and cannot possibly grasp the depth of love so truthful. O, how can he understand? For his youth is a memory long abandoned, but I am in the thick of mine, and youth is a quick, bright thing. This love, I believe, is sanctioned by the stars.

What can it matter that I know nothing of her, other than that she loves me too? I may not know her favorite flower, her favorite ballad, or the day and month of her birth, or whether or not she can read. We have not seen the snow together. We have not even shared the rain. But one hot night upon her balcony has proved enough for both of us.

The friar chided me, and warned me. But, praise the angels, he did at last consent to deliver the sacrament when it occurred to him that our happy alliance might be the only salve sufficient to soothe Verona's wounds.

Before the sun has set this day, a secret wife fair Juliet shall be
With whispered vows I shall become husband to my beloved enemy.

BENVOLIO

I awaken there upon the mossy ground, Rosaline
beside me.

'Tis nearly daylight. Her satiny cheek rests upon my
chest, her hair tumbling o'er my shoulders, her breaths
coming in time with my heartbeat. God's truth, I would
stay forever, but a moment later, she opens her eyes and
recollects our whereabouts.

She bolts to her feet, inadvertently using my rib cage
as a springboard. I utter a strangled "ummph!" and clutch
my middle.

Rosaline has gone pale, nearly as pale as I, who am
struggling for a blessed breath. I attempt to calm her
with a word but can manage only an airless grunt, which

she ignores, unaware that she has pounded the wind from my lungs.

"O, Benvolio! What have we done?"

"We have slept," I manage, rolling over onto my knees and standing slowly. "Prior to that, we but talked. I swear to thee, nothing more."

She frowns in confusion. "Art thou certain?"

I grin at her. "Art thou not?"

Rosaline ponders a moment. "I remember . . . falling."

"As do I," I tell her. *In love*, I add silently. *With you.* "We found the moss most comfortable, so we remained there upon it, looking up through the leaves and twigs at the stars."

The color returns to her complexion, her eyes show relief. "Aye, we talked. Of many things. Of my desire to become a healer. Of Mercutio's legendary temper and the prince's politics." She smiles now. "And of your secret fear of very high places."

"Which you promised ne'er to mention to a living soul outside these woods."

" 'Twas wonderful talk," she says on a sigh. "I now know your favorite color is emerald—"

"And I know that you did accept the existence of fairies until the eve of your twelfth birthday, when Tybalt told you they were naught but fantasy."

She laughs, and the sound fills the forest in a way that makes me wonder if there might be fairies after all.

"I especially liked the story of how you and Romeo once stole a quince tart from the village baker's shop!"

"We were but seven summers," I remind her. "And that thievery is nothing compared to what you and Juliet attempted yesterday in Montague's garden!"

"Thievery?" she repeats, eyes glimmering. "Nay, 'twas just a prank!" Of a sudden, her expression turns sad. "I recall as well that we spoke also of how deeply you mourn for your late mother."

"I have ne'er spoken of that," I tell her, "to anyone."

She steps forward to place a sweet kiss upon my cheek. "I thank you for trusting me."

We begin to walk, enjoying one another's reticence. I can hear the sounds of the town in the distance, coming awake, but I pay them no heed. A plot has begun to arrange itself in my mind, a ploy that might, should the heavens wish to smile upon Verona, put an end to the infernal feud that has kept me thus far from knowing Rosaline. If the elders cannot bend in their beliefs, then perhaps 'tis up to us, their progeny, to be the wiser.

We reach the grove's boundary, stepping into the unshaded daylight, thick with heat. In the sunlight, the blue of her eyes is nearly too pure to be real. Before I reveal my plan, there are two things I must know.

"Speak true, lady. Dost thou still believe thyself to fancy Mercutio?"

Rosaline nibbles her lower lip. I realize I am holding my breath, awaiting her reply.

"I do not," she says at last.

I would take her in my arms there and then but dare not. Instead, I clear my throat and inquire, "What of Romeo? Wouldst thou think me disloyal if I—"

"Romeo?" She smiles. "Oh. I did not have the chance to tell you. Romeo's affections are now engaged elsewhere."

"Art thou certain? Why, only yesterday the boy was racked with despair o'er your refusal to love him."

"He has met another," she informs me. "One he loves better."

I suppose I am smiling like an idiot now, for this news removes the only obstacle to my pursuit of this celestial creature. I am more confident now than ever in my plan.

"Get thee home," I advise, for I want too much to kiss her. "May I see you anon?"

"You may," she says. "Then again, you may not."

"Now, there is a risk I do not wish to take. Let us confirm a plan to assure me of your company."

"Name the place."

"The tavern called the Untamed Shrew."

"I am not familiar with the establishment."

"I did not expect you would be. It is an unseemly sort of pub, not at all suited to ladies of your ilk. But I have conceived of an idea."

She smiles, amused and trusting. "Pray, what manner of scheme would lure me to such a compromising haunt as this Untamed Shrew?"

"You are as eager to end the feud as I, are you not?"

She nods.

"My strategy is this—I will bring Mercutio to the tavern around midday. You will arrange somehow for Tybalt to arrive there then as well. At that time, you and I shall make our announcement."

She lifts one slender eyebrow. "And which announcement might that be?"

"That we are affianced."

Her pretty mouth drops open at the thought of such a sudden escalation in our relationship. But, thanks be to God, she does not say no to matrimony straightaway! Finally, she finds her voice.

"Are you . . . ," she stammers. "Dost thou . . . is this . . . a proposal of marriage?"

"Not remotely," I reply.

"And yet you say we are to be wed?" My beautiful, intelligent Rosaline needs only a moment to comprehend. "Ah, yes! 'Tis a brilliant scheme. If Tybalt and Mercutio believe that we are to be married, they will be compelled to accept that the Capulets and Montagues are family." She clasps her hands together and beams at me, going on in a rush of understanding and excitement. " 'Tis a perfect inroad! The Montagues and Capulets, believing that they are to be united by the holiest of sacraments, will have no choice but to cease their warfare! Indeed, as you and I are enemies once removed, being merely the niece and nephew of the primary combatants, our union would not cause the sort of outrage that would, say, the marriage of Romeo and Juliet, who are the most direct heirs to the hatred. The umbrage to such as that would be insurmountable. However, our union, being peripheral to the heart of the grudge, shall present a case for peace in such a way that neither side will need admit defeat."

"Honor demands that family doth not kill family," I add. "Even Mercutio, who scorns the concept of honor and, moreover, is not of Montague blood, will surely refrain from killing his great friend's future cousin."

"And Tybalt," says Rosaline, "will likely be too concerned with what suit of clothes he should wear to our wedding feast to consider drawing his sword." She rewards me with a smile. "Aye, 'tis brilliant!"

"Then you agree to meet me in the tavern at noon?"

"I do!"

Those words from her lips cause my heart to thud. We walk on toward the square, her pretty lips quirked in a thoughtful way.

"I am curious, sir. Dost thou entertain the idea of a real marriage one day?"

I nod in reply.

"How dost thou suppose you would do it?" she asks, in a tone more academic than romantic. "Propose, I mean."

"I can tell thee for certain that when I feel worthy enough to ask a lady for her hand in earnest, it shall include a wealth of kisses, moonlight, and myself on bended knee offering a gem of inordinate size and a promise of love to last the duration of my life."

Her sweet gasp pleases me much.

"And what of you?" I inquire, inclining my head to mask my interest. "Surely you wish to be proposed to in a most magnificent and ceremonious manner?"

To my great shock, the lady shakes her head. "I told you yesterday, I have no wish to marry."

Has someone just thrust a dagger into my heart? God's blood, it feels as though someone has. "You also told me yesterday that Mercutio altered that particular perception."

"He did," she admits. "Temporarily. And look you how such a deviation ended, with me toppling from a balcony." Her speech slows now to a pensive pace. "And you appearing in time to catch me . . . our night spent in the grove, a discussion of slow kisses . . ."

Again, she shakes her head, this time as though to clear it of such thoughts. Her pretty hair tumbles in the sunlight and she smiles, a bit guardedly. "Our faux betrothal will be more than enough for me. And once the town has forgotten the feud, we shall confess that it was, in fact, only a hoax."

That is not the way I envisioned it. I walk on in silence. As we near the market square, I realize there will be enough townspeople already about to warrant some discretion. " 'Twould be a severe blow to your reputation for us to be seen together at this hour."

"Yes," she agrees. " 'Twould be prudent for us to part company here."

But neither of us moves.

Now something occurs to me. "How wilt thou lure Tybalt to the tavern?"

"It will be simple." Her eyes sparkle mischievously. "I will tell him a most outrageous lie." Before she can explain, we hear the sound of footsteps drawing near. "Anon, good Benvolio."

With a wink, Rosaline lifts the hem of her skirt and hurries off. She has just rounded the corner of the church when Romeo's servant, Balthasar, appears.

He has news for me.

And it is grave.

ROSALINE

I have never considered myself the tavern-wench sort. 'Tis comical, verily, this ploy of mine to bring Tybalt to the Untamed Shrew today. I have instructed my maid-servant, Marie, to deliver him a missive explaining that I have, of all things, accepted a position at the disreputable inn, and this very noon hour I shall begin my first shift as a barmaid there. (I am counting on Tybalt's quick temper to stave his good sense. In truth, there is no logical purpose for a noble-born lady such as I to seek employment anywhere.) I also writ there have oft been known to be hooligans gathered there, and I would be very much grateful for his protection. Marie is to bring him the letter no earlier than a quarter before that hour, which shall ensure his timely arrival.

Indeed, I wonder what will stun my protective cousin more—the news that I have become a barmaid or the news that I shall become a Montague!

'Twill be only an act, of course. I will be no more a wife than a waitress. We will only pretend to be engaged, Benvolio and I. This wells up a strange feeling in me, one I cannot name. But before I can think more deeply on't, there comes a knock upon my door and Juliet bursts into my chamber, flushed and smiling for all she is worth.

"Congratulate me, cousin!" she cries, throwing herself into my arms.

I comply, though I know not for what I am congratulating her. She squirms free of the hug and retreats a step, allowing me to admire her as she spins like a giddy dancer.

"Do I look changed at all?" she inquires.

"Aye, most assuredly," I tell her, for it is true. Juliet this morn appears more . . . well . . . more thoroughly *Juliet* than ever before, though in a way I cannot precisely describe. "Thou hast not changed thy hair. And you wear a gown I have seen you in at least one time before. Art thou taller—thinner—since last night? Pray tell what brings about this remarkable transformation, for indeed, that is surely what it is."

Juliet goes up on tiptoe and cups her hand to my ear to whisper something, but her excitement blows the words out in an unintelligible rush.

"Buried?" I repeat the word I think she spoke. "Say you

that you have been *buried* this morning? Jules, that is non-sense."

She rolls her eyes. "I did not say buried, cousin. I said . . ." Again, she leans in and whispers.

And this time I hear her clearly.

"Married?"

She nods, her eyes bright with the thrill of it. Her delight proves momentarily contagious.

"Married," I gasp in disbelief. "To Romeo, I assume?"

"You assume correctly." She twirls, laughing. "O, I am a wife! I am wife to Romeo! He is my husband!"

"Aye. But how . . . ?"

"He sent word with my nurse, inviting me to our wedding. Naturally, I accepted and did hasten to the monastery, where Friar Laurence did close our hands with holy words. I am married, Roz! 'Tis full real, and duly blessed. I belong to Romeo, and Romeo is mine!" Again, she twirls.

I would dance with her, but 'tis now that the magnitude of the situation settles in. Of a sudden, my mouth goes dry, and my heart begins to pump ferociously. A terror rises within me, a panic so intense I can barely breathe.

"Juliet, you have surely taken leave of your mind! By all that is holy on God's earth, you have signed a death warrant for us all!"

Juliet huffs, pressing her fists to her hips. "You exaggerate. Aye, my father will be angry at first, my mother, shocked. And Romeo's lord and lady will also react badly, but—"

"If by badly you mean slipping a hangman's noose round his handsome neck, then, aye, you have hit the mark. They will never accept you!"

"They must accept us!" Her eyes are glittering with tears now. "I could not bear it if they did not."

"What you can or cannot bear will be of no consequence in the face of their fury. I daresay, you and Romeo have gone too far. Hell's blood, cousin, you are but thirteen. You have known the boy less than a day!"

"Last night you approved." She huffs at me, folding her arms across her chest indignantly.

"I approved of your wanting to love him. Dost thou not recall my warning you to proceed slowly and with caution?"

I take her by the shoulders and push her into a chair, then pull up another and sit facing her. "Ironical as this is going to seem, Benvolio and I had a similar plan. Ours was perilous to some degree, but this rash, impulsive thing that you have done is nothing short of tragic. Each family will blame the other for such colossal injury. Your father will feel betrayed, as will Romeo's. The wrath this marriage will unleash is unimaginable."

There is a long pause. Then Juliet lifts her chin in a childish gesture. "Well, it is done. Romeo and I have sealed our love, and with it our fate."

I consider the news, and I wonder how it will impact the course Benvolio and I had hoped to take. Certainly, our cousins' truth makes our falsehood unnecessary. I cannot suppress the prickle of regret that comes with this realization.

"Well, I suppose this marks the sudden end to my career as a tavern wench."

Juliet looks at me as though I am mad.

"Pay it no mind," I tell her. " 'Tis a long story."

Now a worried crease mars Juliet's brow. "Speaking of long stories," she begins in a tremulous voice, "I was hoping you might explain something to me." She draws a long breath. "I know nothing of what Romeo shall expect of me on our wedding night!"

"Nay." I allow a slight grin. "I suppose you would not."

"Canst thou tell me, Roz? Impart to me some understanding of what a man demands and what a lady ought to do . . . and ought not to do? I know your personal experience is as lacking as mine own. But you are a healer, in essence, a physician. You must know, at the very least, *something*."

She is curious and afraid, and every bit as desperate as she sounds.

I squirm in my seat, a tad stymied by her request. "I know only—how shall I describe it?—only the *mechanics* of the procedure in question. The simple physicality. I can tell you what goes where and why. But with respect to romance, and, well, pleasure—"

"Aye, pleasure. From what little I have heard spoken among my lady's maids and servants, I suspect there is a good deal of pleasure to be had."

"Must be," I mutter, more to myself than to Juliet, "for so many seem so eager to partake in it."

"If Romeo's kissing is any indication of what follows, then I am sure it will not be entirely awful."

A pang of envy strikes me, as I remember Benvolio's failed attempt upon that unsteady log—*a kiss unkissed, and sorely missed.*

"I know this much," I tell her. "You have done well to stay your desires until after your wedding, for when undertaken outside the sanctity of wedlock, the love act often has dire consequences."

Juliet considers this. "I suppose, then, 'tis a good thing that we married so quickly. I daresay I would have been hard-pressed to maintain my virtue otherwise."

I recall the sweet surprise of waking up in Benvolio's arms and know she speaks the truth. "Chances are, Romeo has had experience with this sort of thing."

"Do you think so?"

"He is a man, after all. He is likely an old hand at this mating thing."

Juliet is appalled. Instantly, I regret the remark.

"Then again, he may be as virginal as you and I. You need know only this: If you truly love Romeo and he adores you as deeply as you say and you are already blessed in the sacrament of matrimony, then there is no wrong way to do . . . what it is you are going to . . . do."

"Will it pain me, do you know?"

"Yes. Most assuredly."

"And will he get me with child on the first try?"

"Mayhap. That is dependent upon your cycle, upon the level of your fertility at this time."

Juliet smiles at the possibility. "A Montague babe in a Capulet womb. Romeo's lord and my own sharing a grandchild! Would that not put an end to the feud?"

I do not answer. For I fear it is equally likely that a child of Montague and Capulet blood would inspire enough heartbreak to bring about the greatest violence yet.

Still she must know what she must know. And so, with cautious candor I impart to her the facts as thoroughly as can one virgin to another.

Abruptly, I wrap my arms around Juliet in a firm embrace.

"God be with you, cousin," I whisper.

God be with us all.

BENVOLIO

Mercutio is in fine form this day. He leads his motley band of fellows through the streets in search of argument. They laugh, taunt, and curse, shoving one another in the name of brotherhood. I imagine Mercutio's head is spinning still with the dregs of last night's drunkenness and that his heart is stinging still from having turned away Rosaline.

"I pray thee, good Mercutio, let's retire," I urge. "The day is hot, the [Capulets] abroad, and if we meet, we shall not scape a brawl; for now, these hot days, is the mad blood stirring." I indicate the tavern, the Untamed Shrew, a few steps off.

He looks at me with bloodshot eyes; his mind is muddy. We enter the tavern.

Within, I immediately search the dusky place for Rosaline.

She is not present as yet, but I have no doubt that she is on her way.

My mind returns briefly to the letter shown to me by Balthasar. 'Twas writ to Romeo by Tybalt, who did spot Romeo at last night's feast and would now challenge Romeo for the insult. Glad am I that Romeo is not about, for if Tybalt were to find him here at the tavern, he would surely demand satisfaction. But the stars align for us. Romeo's present absence will allow my plan to play out in peace. Hopefully 'twill be the beginning of the end of violence in Verona.

TYBALT

I have only just come awake—'tis perhaps an hour before noon, by the way the slants of sunlight come blistering into my chamber—when I notice the girl lingering in the courtyard of my father's home.

Her back is to me, but I recognize her to be Rosaline's maid, the one with the remarkable ginger-colored curls and sweet giggle. I admire her a moment before addressing her through the window.

"Good morrow, pretty one."

She spins away from the topiary she's been examining, startled by the closeness of my voice. (My rooms are situated on the house's main level. As such, my window is somewhat near to the ground.)

She offers a curtsy. "Good morrow, my lord."

"Marie, is it?" I fold my arms upon the windowsill and smile out at her. "Pray tell, what brings thee to my garden, Marie?"

She rises from her genuflection, her ringlets bobbing, her deep brown lashes fluttering. "Sir, I am to deliver you a message from my lady."

"Are you, now? Well, surely I must remember to thank my dear cousin for sending me a most adorable messenger." I extend my hand through the window opening, crooking my finger in a beckoning manner.

Wide-eyed, she draws nearer. Her pretty chin comes even with the window sash. With a wink, I tap my forefinger upon her dainty nose, then catch one of her enticing pink-gold curls gently round my thumb.

"My lady did instruct me to deliver the message at a particular hour," she informs me. " 'Tis not yet time, which is why I have been waiting here in the garden."

"You are as conscientious as you are charming." Her blush encourages me. I lean farther out the window toward her. "As it seems you have some time to kill, may I insinuate myself into your fine company?"

Her lips part in surprise. Ah, and then that giggle . . .

"I shall take that to mean yes."

In moments, I have ducked out the window and dropped into the garden, where Marie obligingly flings her lovely self into my arms.

ROSALINE

I send Juliet home to think upon her wedding night and hurry out into the hot day. I must prevent Tybalt's arrival at the Untamed Shrew and apprise Benvolio of this drastic alteration in our plan. 'Tis only half past eleven. My maid is not due to deliver my communiqué to Tybalt for a quarter hour yet.

I will hasten to Tybalt's home, intercept the message, and continue on to the Untamed Shrew to confer with Benvolio.

'Twill be simple.

O, 'tis not simple at all!

Damn Tybalt! Damn his roguish charm!

I arrive at my cousin's house to find Marie sobbing in the rear courtyard. Sobbing and quite nearly undressed.

"Marie! What in God's name is the matter? Where is Tybalt?"

She lifts her guilty eyes to me, producing a shower of fresh tears. " 'Twas not my fault, Lady Rosaline. On my oath, I did endeavor to follow your directive faithfully."

"But Tybalt had other plans?"

She nods. I fold my arms across my chest and frown. "Tell me precisely what hath occurred."

"Well, you see, my lady, I arrived nearly a full hour prior to the time you bid me give your cousin the missive. I could see him within, for his window is low. He was still abed and sleeping. O, he did sleep sweetly, his handsome face made even more beauteous in repose, and of course, his torso was bare and perfect—"

"Marie!"

"Aye. He . . . he was asleep. As I dared not to awaken the gentleman, I loitered here in the courtyard. I was quiet, lady, I swear it, but he awoke nevertheless. 'Twas as though he was aroused by my very presence—"

"*Marie!*"

"Aye, aye . . . he awoke and beckoned me to his window."

I let out a long sigh, for I know where this is going.

"The next I knew, he had removed himself from his chamber by way of the window, and then he led me to yon bench and began to kiss me. Naturally, I returned his kisses—"

"Naturally."

"And naturally, his hands did begin to, well, roam . . . and, quite by accident, one of those gentle, manly hands of his slid into my pocket, although I do believe 'twas not my pocket he was aiming for."

I nod slowly, my eyes narrowed. "And while that manly-and-so-forth hand of his was in thy pocket, he discovered the missive."

"Aye, my lady. And he read it." Her voice breaks suddenly on a sob. "And . . . and . . . 'twas then that he *stopped* kissing me!"

With that, she dissolves into tears. I wish I could spare a moment to console her, but time is short. I give her a hasty pat upon her shoulder, then turn and rush from the garden, knowing one thing for certain:

If I do not get to the Untamed Shrew in time, blood will be shed.

PART TWO

TYBALT

I came upon the Montagues in the very place where Rosaline's letter said she was to be employed as a barmaid. I was dressed perfectly for some cheerful violence in a fine green tunic, donning my best-loved cap, the scarlet velvet with its stiff plumage of raven feathers.

Swordplay, 'twas all it was, I swear it.

Swordplay, and arrogance, and honor, and heat, all combined to take a life. Men as boys on a summer's day, swinging danger in an arc, balancing hatred on a rapier's blade.

And in the midst of all that bluster, Romeo did beg for peace. He turned his back to me, a gesture of trust. He e'en enlisted Benvolio's level head and courageous hand in putting an end to the combat. Down deep, I think I would have welcomed the respite, but I did not wish to be the one to relent.

So we fought, Mercutio and I. Well-matched, we were, till Romeo did intercede, coming betwixt Mercutio and me to shield his friend. At the sight of that, I did boil with envy, for I knew that in all the world I had not one friend who would do the same for me.

'Twas then I thrust the weapon that found its way 'neath Romeo's arm to Mercutio's heart.

On my oath, 'twas as if the point of my own sword had punctured me as well. I felt it pierce some part of me unprotected by skin. And I ran . . . though I soon returned.

My fellows urged me stay away, but I could not bring myself to do so. The image of Romeo's back turned to me, the knowledge that he had offered me faith, did impel me to this place.

This place where I killed Mercutio.

This place where now I lie dying.

Truly, I had come back only to profess my regret as well as my culpability, though I knew that e'en my most sincere contrition would fall sadly short. For Romeo was beyond sense—he thought I came to boast, and knowing me, who could blame him?

We fought.

I fell.

And Romeo fled.

He believed that wrong to be his right. But no murder

is of value, no kill worthwhile. I pray Romeo will one day learn that truth.

Presently, the citizens come in righteous fury, calling for the prince.

O, in what will they dress me for my funeral? I pray they bury me in good style. My breath comes so small; still, I am still not still.

O, Death doth stalk me slowly.

When will come that final, guilty breath with which to end my story,
To let my soul depart and chase Mercutio's to heaven, to our
undeserved glory?

ROMEO

O, I am a fool! Fortune has made me her plaything! For Tybalt lies dead. Tybalt, my wife's cousin, dead at my own hand.

How Fortune laughs to see me tremble!

I came upon them, fresh from my wedding. My cousin Benvolio, Mercutio my good friend, and Tybalt, newly mine own kin.

Then Tybalt did slay Mercutio, and I slew Tybalt.

Benvolio commanded I take my leave, reminding me of the prince's wrath.

And so I escape, knowing this:

'Twas a senseless fight, a fair and graceful fight, inspired by every emotion to which man is prone.

Romeo

Mostly love and mostly hate.
O, I am fortune's fool!

For in my heart, I did never mean to murder Tybalt,
but Tybalt now is dead.
Love's put her lusty dagger in my soul, as sure as the prince shall
put a bounty on my head.

MERCUTIO

Dying is sweeter than anger, kinder than love. 'Tis a state of perfect ease and loneliness. 'Tis bliss and sadness, all as one.

Dying, I depart myself, ghostly aware, released from flesh and form to linger here but a little way above their heads, their blessed, cursed heads!

But the day goes on—how odd! Hath the universe forgotten me already? The world concerns itself with only those who live, and Mercutio lives no more! Worms' meat am I! Young, and gone.

Dying, I mourn my own fierceness and all those petty losses.

Here in the hot sky, I am as vaporous as vanity, as airy as honor. I am nothing.

Mayhap, I was nothing all along.

And now some splendid force does tug upon my nothingness, guiding me higher. O, in dying I am forgiven, but even forgiven, I cannot forgive them that live.

Aye, a plague upon the Montagues, a scourge upon the Capulets! 'Tis what they deserve, and if heaven will not have me, I shall find another place.

Tybalt did remove me of my life. Romeo helped. He came between us, and I was hurt under his arm. Tybalt's sword, it seems, is more ferocious than friendship.

As proof, see there my earthly remains. I bleed from near my heart.

But then, I always did.

And now the sky accepts me; earth recedes, I meet the sun.
Dying becomes death at last, and I am done.

ROSALINE

I run.

My slippers pound the dust, loosening my braid so that my hair escapes in wanton spirals around my face. At my nape, the long curls dampen with perspiration.

I run harder.

For if Tybalt gets to the tavern before me, tragedy will assuredly ensue.

Recalling Benvolio's directions, I hurry past the cemetery toward the outskirts, and soon find myself entering the disreputable section of Verona. Saints in heaven, was I to go left or right at the old coppersmith's shop? O, which is it? *A destra? Sinistra?*

I choose right, and correctly, for I come to the rusting water pump. According to Benvolio, the Untamed

Shrew is but two narrow streets east of here. I run harder still.

And now I hear crying coming from the shadows of a decaying livery stable.

My heart lurches at the sound of it, so desperate is it to mine ears. I stop running and approach the noise. The stable's door has long since been torn asunder. I enter and glance round, my eyes adjusting to the gloom as I search out the source of such sobbing.

'Tis a child, huddled in a rotting hay bale. God's blood, it is young Viola! I hasten to her side, to kneel beside her.

She flinches, looking up at me with terror-filled eyes. "Rosaline!"

The child flings herself into my arms and sobs even more deeply than before.

"O, what is it, darling one?" I ask. "Are you lost, hurt?"

"Lost and hurt," she says into my shoulder. "The whores took me."

My stomach goes sour at the thought of it.

"They tied my hands." Trembling, she extends her arms so I might see them.

The sourness in my belly turns to out-and-out pain. Her wrists are bleeding, rubbed raw from the rope used to bind them. Immediately, I sweep aside my heavy skirt and set to tearing off a wide portion of my undersmock.

Thankfully, that action causes Viola to give over terror for curiosity. She watches intently, her breaths coming in shudders, and I will my voice to be calm as I continue to speak, all the while gently wrapping her tender wounds.

"How did these people take you?" I ask.

"It was night. Sebastian was coughing. I tried to pat his back like you did, but it only helped for a moment."

I am momentarily amazed that such a young child would be astute enough to notice and remember such a thing. I nod and give her an encouraging smile.

"I got up to get him a cup of water, but the ewer was empty. I had to come to the pump."

I finish with the bandage but do not let go of her small hand.

"The whores were drinking wine, and they called out to me and said I would make a fine harlot, for I'm prettier than all of them. I told them I was but ten summers, and they laughed and said there were men aplenty who would pay a pile of silver to have an untried maiden like myself."

God's truth, I could retch right here. I squeeze her hand.

"That is when they caught me and bound my wrists."

"How didst thou get away?" I ask, my voice tight with revulsion.

She draws a deep breath. "They brought me to a pub, a filthy place where there were more bad women and men who reeked of ale. They stood me upon a table and offered me to whosoever bid the highest price." Her words come flatly, but her eyes are brimming with tears.

"I remember a good amount of shouting, and finally a

crippled man offered two gold coins for me. He could hardly walk, so one of the whores dragged me outside for him. He hobbled toward the alley, and she shoved me along behind him. O, Rosaline, I was frightened. He was old and ugly, and he had a gnarled hand to match his ruined leg. When the harlot took her leave, I thought I might faint from panic."

She pauses to collect herself. I am almost unwilling to hear what happened next, but I must, for depending upon the cripple's treatment of her, she may have need of the Healer.

"What happened then?" I prod softly.

Now her expression turns to one of disbelief. "He used his good hand to unbind my wrists," she whispers. "And then he told me to run."

"Run?" I repeat, astonished.

"Run away, he said. He told me he was sorry he could not bring me to safety himself, but his disfigurement pre-vented it. Before I could depart, another man appeared in the alley. He lunged for me, knocking the cripple to the ground. The vile man had me backed against the wall and he was about to—"

Again, I squeeze her hand, wishing dearly it were that vicious lecher's throat.

"'Twas then I heard the barking."

"Barking?"

Viola nods. "Barking. And growling. 'Twas a dog who had been sleeping in the alley. A very old dog."

My eyes widen in amazement. "Crab!"

"Yes, 'twas Crab! Benvolio feeds him, and once he brought Crab to play with us. Crab jumped at the bad man, and tore into him with his teeth. The man fell hard, dead, I think, and the cripple yelled, 'Run, child!' so I did."

I am silent for a moment as I pray for all God's blessing upon that brave and faithful stray, and ask Him to watch o'er the pure heart of the crippled stranger.

"Viola, I shall see you home by and by, but first I've an errand I must undertake. Can you walk?"

She gains her feet, still clutching my hand, and we hurry out into the blazing sunlight, to the Untamed Shrew.

"Rosaline?"

"Aye?"

"I would like to give you something. A gift."

"'Tis not necessary—"

"Please. 'Twould make me glad if I could give to you what I count most precious in this world. For I know you will love this gift near as much as I."

"In that case, I will be honored to have it." I smile down at the pretty child. "Pray, what is this thing you love most that you wish me to have?"

Her very heart is in her eyes when she answers.

"Benvolio."

We arrive in the thick of a crowd. Townspeople and nobles have gathered in this spot where I was to meet Benvolio. The shouting and sobbing do not bode well, though here, at the back of the throng, I cannot make out what has occurred. People shiver though it is sweltering. Others seem numb and affrighted. O'er their heads in the distance I can see the tavern's shingle reading THE UNTAMED SHREW and the prince aloft, speaking grimly to the citizenry from the tavern's high steps.

I hold tight to Viola and shoulder through to the front of the mob.

Alas, I come too late.

For hither in the street before the empty tavern lie Mercutio and Tybalt.

O, the sight is torture to behold. Tybalt, my dear cousin and adored friend, sprawled motionless upon the ground. Even in his teasing did he express his love of me. And ever did he seek to protect me, to teach me, to make me laugh. My sudden grief renders me absurd, and I can only think how disturbed my vain and darling cousin would be to see his fine clothing smudged with blood and dirt.

And near to him lies Mercutio. A rake, aye, but e'en the most troublesome lad does not deserve to die in the beauty of his youth. O, I would weep for this waste, but I cannot, for I am too afraid of what worse will come because of it.

Benvolio is near the prince on a lower step, relaying the tale of woe. The loathsome account assails my ears in Benvolio's beauteous voice.

"*An envious thrust from Tybalt hit the life of stout Mercutio, and then Tybalt fled; but by and by comes back to Romeo, who had but newly entertain'd revenge, and to't they go like lightning, for, ere I could draw to part them, was stout Tybalt slain; and as he fell, did Romeo turn and fly."*

He turns to the crowd, his hand upon his heart, his expression sober. *"This is the truth,"* he concludes darkly, *"or let Benvolio die."*

I cannot imagine the prince would think Benvolio's report dishonest. Then I understand that 'tis not for the prince's benefit he's made that final avowal. I see his eyes fixed upon my aunt, Lady Capulet. She is glaring at him as though he himself did murder her nephew. I would throw myself betwixt her and Benvolio simply to shield him from her hateful stare. O, can she not see the grief in Benvolio's gaze, his vast regret, his genuine hurt?

"He is a kinsman to the Montague," she shrieks in abhorrence, *"affection makes him false, he speaks not true. . . . I beg for justice, which thou, Prince, must give: Romeo slew Tybalt, Romeo must not live."*

I feel Viola tug upon my sleeve. "Rosaline—"

"Hush, please," I implore her, not taking my eyes from Benvolio.

She tugs again, but Montague hollers, *"Not Romeo, Prince, he was Mercutio's friend; his fault concludes but what the law should end, the life of Tybalt."*

The prince does silent battle with this logic. Again, Viola pulls upon my dress.

"Look you, Rosaline, that one—"

I shake my head at her and touch my finger to her lips. There is something urgent in her eyes, but I cannot address it now for I am missing the sovereign's decree. "You may tell me anon," I promise in a whisper. "I must listen to the prince."

The child presses her lips shut obediently. I turn my attention back to the prince, as Viola bounces beside me in an agitated manner.

"Let Romeo hence in haste," the prince announces somberly, *"else, when he's found, that hour is his last. . . ."*

My heart sinks at this dire declaration for 'tis Juliet's doom as well.

Now the prince instructs that the bodies be removed. The people disperse quickly. The prince departs as well, followed by his agents. I watch my aunt take her leave and understand that she goes directly to call forth servants who will prepare the Capulet tomb for Tybalt's interment. My mind whirls in tumult. This morning, a secret wedding; this night, a public funeral.

When no one remains but Viola and myself with Tybalt and Mercutio dead at our feet, I turn to Benvolio, who is coming down the steps to draw me into his arms.

"I'm sorry," I utter. "If only I had arrived more expeditiously. If only—"

"Shhhh, angel. 'Tis not your fault. This date was long in coming. You could not have stopped them any more than I."

"But if I had just—"

Now Viola has taken a handful of my skirt and pulls with all her might. "Rosaline!" she wails.

I turn away from Benvolio, remembering she had wished fervently to tell me something earlier. "Aye, Viola. You are indeed a patient lady, and I commend you on that. Now, dear one. Tell me what the matter is."

"That one," she squeaks, pointing her finger at Tybalt, lying face down in the hard dirt. "Look you at that one."

Benvolio lowers his eyebrows. "What of him?" he asks.

Viola looks direct at me and nods. "He breathes."

BENVOLIO

The child speaks true.

Tybalt breathes!

I crouch beside him, withdraw my dagger, and place the shining steel blade beneath his nose; a slight exhalation fogs the reflective metal.

He bleeds, but aye, he is breathing yet.

Rosaline examines Tybalt's wound with deft skill. 'Tis not nearly as deep as it looks," she tells me, "and he was not struck in a critical place. Romeo's sword did merely pierce my cousin's flesh. E'en had it penetrated farther, 'twould have missed his organs completely."

"Why then does he not move?" I ask.

"I am not certain," she admits. "But the Healer will

know." She turns to Viola. "Sweet child, wilt thou do something for me? Something important."

Viola nods determinedly.

"Know you where to find the Healer's cottage?" Rosaline asks.

Again, the child nods.

"Get thee there at once." She gives Viola a serious look to communicate the gravity of the task. "Tell the Healer that we are bringing to her a patient and that she must make ready for his arrival."

"I shall run all the way!" With that, Viola turns and bolts, running as swiftly as her little legs can carry her.

I stand, lifting Tybalt and slinging him as carefully as possible o'er my shoulder. We set out for the Healer's cottage.

"Know you what this means?" Rosaline asks. "Romeo can no longer be charged as a murderer! The prince will be obligated to recant his exile."

"There is truth in that, however . . ." I sigh, unwilling to trample on her optimism. "That surely will not be the end of it. Should Tybalt recover, I am sure the Montagues will only demand his prompt execution for having killed Mercutio."

Rosaline thinks on this. Deep in contemplation, her brilliant mind turning, she is even more beautiful to me.

"Then I myself shall appeal to his Majesty on the issue," she says at last. "Surely God has not kept Tybalt alive only to allow him to be executed! But you are right—the

Montagues will demand satisfaction, so for now we must not reveal that Tybalt remains among the living. The Healer can hide him in her cottage and tend to him there."

"But the undertaker is on his way. He will have been told to expect two corpses."

Again, Rosaline works the problem in her mind. "I am fairly certain the mortician has ne'er seen my cousin up close. Therefore, he will accept whatever dead body he finds beside Mercutio's to be that of Tybalt of the house of Capulet."

"How is that helpful?" I ask her, motioning to where Mercutio lies alone. "The undertaker will still find himself short one cadaver."

"No, he will not," Rosaline tells me.

"And your kinsmen, won't they wonder—"

"Leave it all to me," she says. "You bring Tybalt to the Healer. I shall meet you at the cottage as soon as I am able."

"As you wish."

"O, and after the Healer has seen to Tybalt, please have Viola describe to her Sebastian's symptoms. Mayhap she can prepare a tonic for the child."

For a moment, I just stare at her, forgetting the weight of Tybalt upon me, ignoring the sadness I feel o'er the loss of Mercutio. For all I can think upon is the fact e'en in the face of such dire circumstance, my angel Rosaline remembers a poor, sick child.

I cannot help myself.

I kiss her soundly on the mouth.

ROSALINE

I follow the stench to the dead man.

In this neighborhood, such a feat requires great concentration, for these mean environs do reek malodorously even when there is not a decaying corpse in the vicinity.

I find him in the alley. Crab, Lord love him, did inflict a most thorough wound upon the villain's throat. But clearly the punishment did not cease there. The condition of his visage indicates that the rats did find him in the night and made a feast of his features. His lips have been torn clear off his face. His skin has been pocked and blistered by the rodents' teeth. His nose is shredded to the bone, and his eye sockets are empty but for a viscous, bloody ooze.

Yet I feel no pang of pity. In truth, my initial impulse

is to kick him squarely in the gut and spit upon his fouled remains. Instead, I do what is right and make the sign of the cross o'er him, asking God's forgiveness for his considerable sins and offering a prayer to commend his soul to the perpetual light of heaven (though in my heart, I believe his rightful place is beside Beelzebub in hell).

Having done that, I take hold of him by the armpits, hoist him halfway up, and drag him to the place where Tybalt did not die.

The mortician is too tall, too thin, too pale, and just obtuse enough for my purposes.

His arrival finds me crying, first over Mercutio then crawling on mine hands and knees to weep before the corpse of the faceless imposter. The mortician watches me awhile as I scuttle betwixt the dead.

At last he clears his throat. "Calm thyself, lady," he says in a voice like stone. "So that I may beg information from thee. Know you the names of these dead?"

I look up at him and sob e'en more robustly.

He releases a windy sigh. "This display of oscillating grief much bewilders me. I was made to understand that I would here find two lads of great enmity, each hailing from one of the feuding houses. Tell me, lady, for whom dost thou weep?"

"For both," I wail. "For all."

His brow wrinkles in confusion. "Pray, wouldst thou indicate which of these fallen foes is your brethren?"

"Which one?" I rise from my knees, still sobbing, my fists clenched, my eyes wild. "Which one, you ask? Zounds, sir, I reply to thee that one as well as the other belongs to me, and as well belongs to thee."

His anger flares. "You addlepated girl! 'Tis not possible!"

"Is it not?" I shake my head despairingly. "O, you sorry soul! The doctrine of our blessed church doth teach us well that we are all God's children. Ergo, I do in my most devoted heart believe that both these boys are now in death as ever they were in life my own dear kith and kin."

The undertaker glares at me, biting down hard on his crooked teeth. "Then tell me this: Of these two here dead, which one is Tybalt, claimed in life by the house of Capulet?"

I point to the body I so recently dragged hither. "He there was Tybalt once."

The undertaker looks to the pilfered corpse. "I was told 'twas a sword that killed him. What has happened to wreak such havoc upon his countenance?"

I bite my lip, summoning some plausible falsehood. 'Tis then I notice a sleek, black raven's feather (which I recognize as having once adorned Tybalt's favorite cap) lying upon the dirt beside the anonymous replacement.

"Birds," I answer.

I snatch the feather from the ground and wave it dramatically. "A swarm of them, aye, black ones, and large, swooping down from the sun-bright sky, with talons bared and bills as sharp as the point of Satan's tail. 'Twas swift and sickening to see, sir. They devoured my cousin's face, then as quickly ascended again to the sky like a dark and writhing cloud of purest evil, squawking and cawing, batting their broad wings."

Now I fall toward the mortician. He flinches as he catches me, and I cling to him. The flinch, I expect, is due to the stink of the corpse that lingers upon me. "Good sir, I implore thee, do not allow Tybalt's relations to see him as I have! He was a vainglorious rascal in life, exceedingly proud of his rugged beauty and elegant form. 'Twas one of the things we loved best about him. On my oath, sir, this boy would prefer to suffer evermore in purgatory than be seen in such an unsightly state."

The undertaker considers this, kneeling beside the corpse to examine the mutilated face. "I cannot repair such as this," he mutters.

"Nay, but you can conceal it, can you not? A simple slip of silk, laid softly upon his ruined face—oh, but be sure that the fabric does complement his shroud, for Tybalt was much concerned with fashion."

The mortician nods. "Aye, 'twill be the kind thing, to cover this mess." He rises, brushing the dust from his knees. "With your leave, lady, I shall bear now this boy to my mortuary, to prepare him for his interment. My apprentice will be along by and by with a box in which to collect the other and transport him to the cemetery, as his family has requested no pomp or pageantry."

A shiver passes o'er me. "Say you that Mercutio will merely be stuffed in an ugly coffin and tossed into a hole in the ground?"

"'Tis not fancy," the man allows with an icy expression that is a perverse imitation of a smile, "but 'tis usually effective."

"No!" I stamp my foot. "Call the clergyman immediately so that he may administer the rites. And bring hither your finest casket—satin-lined and trimmed with gilt. I shall myself accept the cost! And see that not one single clot of earth be dropped upon Mercutio until all of the customary prayers have been offered!"

After a moment, he consents with a curt nod of his long head. "Done." With that, the undertaker hoists the nameless corpse from the ground and departs.

When he is gone, I lean down and brush a lock of hair from Mercutio's forehead. "Please endeavor to behave in heaven," I whisper, as a tear escapes my eye. "Flirt not with God's angels! And smile down whene'er you can upon Benvolio, for he shall miss you deeply." I lean closer and place a kiss upon his cheek. "As will I."

Tybalt's raven feather becomes heavy in my hand. At home I will keep it protected within the pages of my Bible. For now, I tuck it into the waistband of my skirt, then rise and hurry away to the Healer's cottage.

BENVOLIO

The Healer sees to Tybalt; she is swift and serious.

Viola watches in fascination as the old woman listens to Tybalt's slight breathing, tugs up one eyelid, then the other, to peer into his sightless eyes. I too am amazed at the scope of her knowledge, the breadth of her compassion.

"Indeed, his body lives," she pronounces gravely. "His lungs do inspire, his heart doth beat. The blood still runs warm in his veins."

"'Tis possible to save him, then?"

The Healer glances at Viola. "Child, prithee, to the garden with thee, and bring me a swath of leafy greens, a stalk of fennel, and the spikey leaves of four dandelion weeds."

Pleased, Viola helps herself to a splintered bushel basket and exits through the back door into the Healer's garden.

"Fennel and dandelion?" I ask. "Ingredients for some manner of medicine?"

The Healer shakes her head. "Ingredients for some salad. The little girl requires her dinner."

"And Tybalt?" I ask quietly. "What doth he require?"

She runs a leathery hand o'er Tybalt's brow and answers, "A miracle."

Rosaline arrives and confers with her mentor.

"So 'twas not Romeo's blade that left good Tybalt in such condition?"

The Healer shakes her head, indicating the gash. "The cut yielded an inconsequential loss of blood." She turns to me. "Thou sayst he fell?"

"Aye," I confirm. "And hard."

"Hard, indeed. For his skull suffered a most acute impact. The damage to his brain is complete and permanent."

"I'd have thought our headstrong Tybalt's skull too thick to incur such an injury." Rosaline bites her lower lip searching for comprehension. "If his brain is ruined, how is it he continues to draw breath?"

"The brain is near as wondrous a mystery as the immortal soul," the Healer explains. "E'en when all capacity for thought has fled, nature and impulse can remain. Tybalt is dead of mind, but his corporeal being still functions. He is here and gone at once, as though he is lost in the deepest of sleeps, a sleep from which he shall ne'er awaken."

I clear my throat. "What, then, are we to do with him?" A chill creeps o'er my flesh, as I consider our various courses. "We cannot bury him alive; 'twould be murder."

"We shall do what we can to nurture what is left," the Healer whispers, "while we wait for the Lord to collect him."

"'Twill not be long, will it?" Rosaline asks in a whisper of her own.

"That is mostly up to God Almighty," the Healer replies, "but partly up to Tybalt's ghost. All depends upon how soon his spirit tires of this strange purgatory. His mind cannot choose, but his soul will decide when 'tis ready to drift away."

I take Rosaline's hand, kiss her cheek. "Mayhap his soul will discover something worthy for which to live."

But from the Healer's pitying expression I understand 'twould be much better were good Tybalt's soul to find something else . . . something worth his death.

ROSALINE

After Viola has had her fill of greens and a large cup-ful of rich goat's milk, Benvolio offers to see her home. In a small burlap pouch she carries a vial of the Healer's best cough elixir for Sebastian. I walk them to the door and bid them good night. They have just rounded the corner of Saint Peter's when I notice a bustling figure of rotund proportions, hastening away from Friar Laurence's cell. 'Tis Juliet's boisterous nurse, Angelica. I beckon her.

"Lady Rosaline?" The nurse lumbers o'er and eyes the Healer's shingle with trepidation. "Why dost thou con-sort with this witch?" she demands in a whisper.

"The Healer is no more a witch than you are," I tell

her. "Now, I would know what Juliet has heard of this day's trouble."

The nurse expels a long sigh. "Aye, aye, this hateful day, endless, hateful day. By my oath, surely the sun has rounded this world more slowly than is customary, or if not, more swiftly, delivering two days in the span of one. O, Lord, this day has seen too much, and I am exhausted from grief." She throws her meaty arms round my neck and commences to sob. "O, Lord, dear Lord! We've lost our Tybalt, our daring, darling Tybalt, the life pierced out of him with a hole put there by none but him who is his cousin's husband. Romeo slew Tybalt! 'Tis a crime unrivaled."

"Has the news been delivered to Romeo's wife?" I ask, still clung to by the nurse.

"'Twas I who told Juliet the news! *Tybalt is gone and Romeo banished, Romeo that kill'd him, he is banished.* Aye, that is exactly how I said it and at last Juliet understood. O, 'twas like a demon burst forth from her breast. She gasped, then she bellowed, then she wailed, and O, how we wept, she in my arms, then I in her arms, and once— just once—she was moved to curse nature for giving her Romeo the spirit of a fiend. In one breath she wished him shame, but in the next, recanted, and deemed Tybalt villain."

I disentangle myself from the nurse's weighty embrace. "What else?"

"What else? I, her devoted companion, did calm her

by promising to bring forth Romeo to console her, that is what else! For though his banishment to Mantua still looms, he remains yet within the bounds of Verona."

"Glad I am to hear he has not departed the city," I say, then wish I hadn't. True, if Tybalt does not die, then Romeo might be spared his sentence. But that is still to be seen, and if the nurse were apprised of e'en the possibility of Romeo's pardon, she might do something rash, and thus complicate things. When the nurse looks at me quizzically, I quickly amend: "So that they may have at least one night together. Where is Romeo at present?"

"I found him in the friar's cell, found him weeping like a woman, writhing on the stony floor as a child would. Ah, well, there is the magnificent truth of it. Aye, 'tis his tender age that is his defect, as Juliet's innocence is hers; they are too green, too childish, too fresh, and unformed in mind and manner for the weight of this love. 'Tis a blessing too burdensome for their scant years to carry. Still, there is nothing for it now, for they are wed and that is sacred. They must grow into this marriage—"

I had forgotten Angelica's tendency to ramble on so. I hold up a hand to silence her. "What did Friar Laurence advise?"

"O, the holy man did have a splendid notion," she replies. "My Juliet and her Romeo shall have their wedding night, for I will hang the corded rope as planned, and Romeo will ascend the ladder to find his bride. Safe they'll be in the cover of night, and on the morrow, before the guard is dispatched, Romeo shall escape to Mantua, where he shalt live till we can find a time to mend this muddle and put it all to rights."

'Tis a sound plan, the only reasonable course. I send the nurse home to report all to Juliet. "Tell my cousin I wish her well. And nurse—"

"Aye, m'lady?"

"Have a care with that corded ladder. Much depends upon it."

She curtsies to me, then turns and ambles away across the square. I send up a silent prayer for Juliet on her wedding night before going back inside the Healer's cottage.

The Healer lights a candle scented with lavender. For a long time, we sit in silence. Tybalt lives, and I watch him with sadness.

" 'Tis frustrating," I say at last, "to see a person suffer and have no ability to aid him." I stand, making my way to the Healer's worktable. Above it are shelves, crowded with herbs and remedies. I examine them, feeling helpless. "There is much we know, much we can cure, and yet—"

"Our profession is young," she tells me. "E'en these many years of study and practice have been insufficient to teach us all this world has to offer in the way of healing. So much is yet unknown, untried. As with Tybalt—I have heard tell of such conditions, but he is the first I've seen myself."

On the scarred wooden surface of the table I spy a wrinkled scrap of paper. A list of ingredients is writ upon it, with fine ink in a careful hand. "What is this?"

"Friar Laurence did bring it to me," she explains, her eyes suddenly wary. "A recipe for some strange liquor, a potion really, sent to him by a learned woman who resides in some land north of here called Denmark. He tells me it carries most astounding properties." Pulling her shawl closer round her shoulders, she describes for me the strange potion's power. "It brings to anyone who ingests it the aspect of death, but in reality 'tis safe to drink as mother's milk. I did brew him one small portion," she confesses.

I shudder. "Seems a profane thing to attempt, sinful almost."

"Aye. I felt so myself, but the friar convinced me 'twas not as bad as all that. But now that he has his experiment, I believe I shall burn the recipe."

She rises slowly from her chair, taking the odious scrap from the table. With steady hand does she hold it above the candle's flame. I watch as the tiny blaze takes hold of the foolscap with flickering yellow teeth, blackening it, curling the edges to ash. At the very last second, the Healer releases the corner she holds, letting it and the small fire that clings to it fall with a hiss upon the tabletop. The flame lasts only a moment, then dies.

After this, we sit in companionable silence, lost in our own thoughts and separate prayers. At last I bid my friend good night and head for home.

I arrive to find my good lady mother in her courtyard. She listens to the music made by steamy breezes in the treetops and the sweetness of crickets' song. I wonder how badly, in these lonesome moments, she does miss the husband who left her, who left us both.

"Rosaline!" my mother calls out. She rushes to me, wraps me in her embrace—I knew not until this moment how much this day of all days I've had need of it. Without warning, I feel the tears begin, slowly at first, but gaining strength until I am sobbing in my mother's arms. These are true and heartfelt. These, at last, are honest tears for Tybalt—who now lives only to decide to die—and for Mercutio.

"God-den, precious one," my mother says, then gives me a soft and serious look. "I looked for thee at Tybalt's funeral this afternoon. Wherefore did you neglect to attend the service? 'Twould have been good for you to bid him farewell. 'Tis the reason we gather o'er our dead—to grieve together, to say good-bye. 'Tis a step toward acceptance."

She is right, of course, but I cannot tell her that the faceless man our family mourned in the tomb this day was not Tybalt.

"I could not bear to witness Tybalt's interment," I explain with a loud sniffle, "for seeing him thus would forever sully my recollection of him. I wished my final memory to be of good Tybalt alive."

She nods in understanding and places her cool palm

upon my cheek. "You look tired. No doubt you and Juliet did not sleep at all last night. Tell me, did you stay up past dawn, giggling and remembering the handsome lords who flirted with thee?"

She laughs lightly, and of a sudden I recall she believes I spent last night at my uncle's house, in Juliet's company. In truth, I spent it talking and snuggling beside Benvolio on the mossy ground of the sycamore grove. Indeed, another thing I cannot tell my mother.

"Did I sleep?" I repeat, sounding more than a bit foolish, then answer honestly, "In fact, I slept very little."

"You girls and your visits. Wherefore dost thou call them sleepovers, I wonder, when you ne'er so much as close your eyes."

Before she can press me further, I excuse myself and hurry indoors. I want nothing more than to say a prayer for Tybalt, then lie down and close my eyes to sleep.

But sleep, again this night, is not to be.

When I arrive in my chamber, I find the window open wide, and there, in a patch of moonlight, waits Benvolio! He places his finger to his lips, bidding me stay quiet.

"How?" I begin softly. "How did you come in?"

"Carefully." He nods toward the open window. "With the aid of a rather unsteady pile of bricks that leads to a low roof, from which I pulled myself in through yon window."

"Resourceful of thee," I whisper.

"Shall I leave?" he asks.

"Never" is my answer. And then I am in Benvolio's arms, and there is no sound but the breezy music of the night without and my name upon his lips.

I will confess, I come awfully close to surrendering my virtue completely, and there is more than one moment when I am nearly unable not to.

But we refrain.

'Twould be a sin, first and foremost, but beyond that, I will not risk getting with child. Benvolio understands. 'Tis wonderful just having the warmth of him here beside me, feeling him breathe, hearing him sigh, kissing him. Soft and slow and lingering.

We sleep, briefly, then awaken to kiss some more. His kisses are perfection. He swears mine are sweeter than any he's ever known, and I believe him, for I have ne'er in my life meant anything as I mean these kisses I give to Benvolio.

When at last we make ourselves say good night, the earliest ribbons of daylight have begun to tease the horizon.

Benvolio slips out the window. I watch him vanish like a sweet dream into the swell of morning, then return to my bed, to sigh myself to sleep.

TYBALT

Upon a downy bed before a cozy fire, in a small, dark cottage, my once able body lies tranquilly. I seem to hover above it, observing from the air. My being is a part of the morning itself.

So I did not die completely, then. I exist there on the soft pallet in a state somewhere in betwixt. Of neither here nor there, life nor death.

'Tis a freedom most frightening, most challenging and intense.

I am a filament, a moment, a thought unthought.

I am trembling nothingness.

'Tis marvelous strange, yet passing pleasant and worth exploring. First, a soundless glide round this quaint dwelling. Ah, there is the woman who keeps a silent vigil.

She is Rosaline's friend, the Healer; I sense her goodness. She approaches, a jar in her wrinkled hands. From here, in the atmosphere, I will my own hands to rise and clutch the woman's arm. But no such movement occurs.

With tender expertise, she dips her withered fingers into the jar and begins to apply a slick salve to the wound upon my chest. I feel nothing. Hath it any scent? I cannot smell—nor do I feel the clean sting it carries, if there is one. Alas, I shall miss sensation quite a lot.

A window. 'Tis open, just a thread's breadth, but that is likely all I need. To the window, then, and out . . .

Out, above the Healer's tidy garden, I mingle with the heat of the coming day. Sunrise is a smudge of apricot color along the horizon—O, for a tunic the color of daybreak! But what use have I for clothing now? For I am more like a morning than a man, I am a smudge of wisdom and sentiment against the sky.

What is expected of me here in the breeze, the bright, the everywhere?

In the distance, I see pebbled country lanes and rough-hewn fences protecting tall tomato gardens, sheep in their pastures, a glistening stream. But I am impelled toward town, and so I soar o'er Saint Peter's spire, skimming *vias*, *piazzas*, and well-kept homes until I come to my uncle's place.

I whisper in, like a dream, through Juliet's open window.

And find myself in hell!

Zounds! That is Romeo she lies with!

That one so young should be abed with *any* man is wrong enough, but of all the bachelors in Verona, she chooses to award herself to *Romeo*?

Romeo, whose weapon left me as I am now. Romeo, in my cousin's bed.

Would that I could shout, I would call for my uncle and all his guardsmen to apprehend this villain! This villain my kinswoman kisses and calls "love."

"Love." She calls him "love."

What can a girl of thirteen summers know of love?

And when in the name of God Almighty did this perversity occur? Before he nicked me with his blade, or since? At the feast? (Saints, was it only one night past? Aye!) Did they make their first acquaintance there, or have they been courting for months and months in secret? Were I not already mostly dead, I believe I might expire from the shock of it!

I alight upon a ledge near her wardrobe and watch as they argue o'er larks and nightingales, and kiss profoundly. Little Juliet, the imp, her hair tousled from a night of—O, God, I wish not to think of what—wrapped in her mother's good sheets and kissing a Montague.

I want to be enraged, but in this wispy state I find that I have more room for forgiveness than fury.

O, fine, then! Juliet may have her Romeo and with my

ethereal blessing. This much is clear, he is her husband, if not in law, then in deed and desire.

From without, her nurse calls, "Madam . . ."

I look on now as Romeo takes his leave. He departs quickly, hastening from the room to the balcony, scaling the outer wall to escape through the orchard. Juliet looks empty in his wake, and afraid.

And now my formidable aunt, Lady Capulet, enters to find her Juliet in tears. Ha, she believes the brat weeps for me!

They talk of my death, and I am lonesome to hear it, but also moved by the extent to which my aunt desires to avenge me.

Juliet lies, of course. She tells her mother she would deliver to Romeo a potion to make him sleep in quiet. Feigning to detest him, she says slyly that her *"heart abhors"* the fact that she canst not *"come to him to wreak the love"* she bore for me upon his body.

Clever girl! If I could laugh, I would, for 'tis cunning of the child to make it sound like a vengeful act, when what in truth she wants to do to that Montague is . . . well, precisely what she has already done upon those sheets. But her cleverness is no shield against what her lady mother announces now: *"Marry, my child, early next Thursday morn, the gallant, young, and noble gentleman Paris, at Saint Peter's church, shall happily make thee there a joyful bride."*

This brings sweet Juliet up short, and her pretty eyes

go bright and sharp and angry when she speaks. "I wonder at this haste, that I must wed ere he that should be husband comes to woo."

So Paris hath not e'en *called* upon her? No wonder she finds insult. Were I still, er, available, I would give Paris a pounding myself! My beauteous cousin most assuredly deserves adequate wooing. Whatever is the matter with my uncle, not to insist the cad come courting before taking as his bride this treasure that is Juliet?

O, the scene worsens now, when Uncle Capulet makes his entrance. He is used to a daughter demure and ever compliant, and his rage ignites when Juliet denies his wish. This change in Juliet stuns me, but in truth, it does what is left of me good to see the urchin show some snap!

Capulet feels otherwise. He calls her unworthy! Juliet, whom just days past he worshipped as the hopeful lady of his earth. Ah, was it merely her weakness that he loved?

I have ne'er seen him so incensed, and now he lashes out at Juliet in such a vicious fashion I cannot help but react, flinging my vaporous being in the path of his ire. 'Tis futile, of course, as I am air. Thankful I am he does not try to strike the girl. Instead, he hurls his cruelty in the form of words.

"*Out, you green-sickness carrion!*" he hollers. "*Out, you baggage!*"

E'en his icy wife is appalled by the severity of his verbal attack. She attempts to intercede, crying "*Fie, fie, what, are you mad?*"

Juliet falls to her knees, but Capulet will hear none from his child and ignores her plea.

"*Wife,*" he growls, "*we scarce thought us blest that God had lent us but this only child, but now I see that this one is one too much, and that we have a curse in having her.*"

O, blister'd be his tongue! Had I wind in me, such wicked words wouldst surely have knocked it out. Juliet, still kneeling, huddles now upon the floor, rocking, shaking with soundless sobs.

And now her nurse does leap to Juliet's defense, daring to speak up to her lord and master. But Capulet's fury subsides not at all. Instead, he hands down a most bruising threat. "*Graze where you will, you shall not house with me. Look to 't, think on 't. I do not use to jest. Thursday is near . . . an you be mine, I'll give you to my friend; and you be not, hang, beg, starve, die in the streets, for, by my soul, I'll ne'er acknowledge thee, nor what is mine shall never do thee good. Trust to 't. . . .*"

Have I heard him rightly? He will toss her out, cut her off from all wealth and comfort! How can he? She is his child. Hath he forgotten that in her infancy he cradled her and thought her more brilliant than the sun? How can this man, my father's brother, this uncle whom I loved and admired, be such a serpent when denied a single want?

Again, poor Juliet begs for reprieve, but Capulet offers none. He goes, and now the girl appeals to her mother, but the woman puts an end to it, taking her own leave with this statement: "*Talk not to me, for I'll not speak a word. Do as thou wilt, for I have done with thee.*"

Is Lady Capulet's heart a thing of ice, that she can abandon her only daughter with words such as these?

Alone with her nurse, Juliet's voice turns as thin as a spinner's web. *"O, God!—O, nurse, how shall this be prevented? What say'st thou?"*

The nurse sighs, and there is a moment of silence before she speaks. And I am harshly amazed by her advice, for 'tis practical, aye, but so unkind, and so verily wrong!

"I think it best you married with the count," says she. *"O, he's a lovely gentleman!"*

Juliet is betrayed again, and by a friend so close as this one. But in pain, she finds resolve, for I mark a slight stiffening of her spine, a lift of her dainty chin. She levels a look at her nurse, and there is something cold in it.

"Well, thou hast comforted me marvelous much," says Juliet. 'Tis an ironical statement, made with sarcasm. The nurse does not recognize it. She smiles, relieved, believing that Juliet has succumbed to her fate.

But I see something brewing there behind my cousin's calm expression, something defiant in her eyes, which belies her sudden agreement.

"Go in and tell my lady I am gone, having displeas'd my father, to Laurence's cell, to make confession and to be absolv'd."

With a nod, the nurse hastens to do it, while Juliet whispers a denunciation in the traitor's wake. "Go, counselor; thou and my bosom henceforth shall be twain. I'll to the friar to know his remedy."

And now, a small, brave smile—had I my body about me, I believe that little grin would cause chills along my spine, and 'tis e'en more certain that had I blood 'twould run cold at the words she utters next.

"If all else fail," say'st Juliet with a most disquieting calm, *"myself have power to die."*

ROSALINE

Late in the afternoon, I arrive at Juliet's. She has sent the nurse's boy, Peter, to summon me; I am told 'tis a matter of dire urgency.

I cannot imagine what could be deemed more dire than what hath already befallen her—a near-dead cousin, a smuggled spouse lately thought a murderer, now banished. I find myself longing for the days when, for Jules, "dire" applied to such circumstances as having no appropriate slippers to wear with a favorite gown.

I make my way through the house noting a great bustle amongst the servants. Lady Capulet and Juliet's nurse are in a fine dither, and mine uncle stands in the center of it all, waving a sheet of paper.

"*So many guests invite as here are writ,*" he instructs a

servant. When that one is dispatched, he catches hold of the sleeve of another and demands, *"Sirrah, go hire me twenty cunning cooks."*

It seems another feast is in the works. Peculiar that a second celebration would come so swiftly upon the coat-tails of the last, and after a death in the family. Ere mine uncle can mark my presence, I make for the stairs and take them in twos.

I reach Juliet's chamber and find the door ajar. "Juliet?"

She jumps at the sound of my entrance and quickly conceals behind her back some small thing she clutches in her fist.

" 'Tis only me, Jules."

"I feared you were my nurse or my lady. They left me just moments ago, bidding me sleep. Ha! As if I could." She tucks the object beneath her pillow now. "O, Roz, glad am I that you have come. 'Tis all so impossibly desperate!"

"What is?"

"Didst thou not notice the commotion in the hall?"

"Aye, it seems your sire plans another banquet."

"Not any banquet. My wedding."

"Your wedding? To whom, for the love of God?"

"Paris," says Juliet, her voice breaking on a sob.

"When?"

" 'Twas set for Thursday, but my anxious lord has changed his mind and called for it to take place tomorrow."

"O, Jules, this is terrible."

"You know not the half of it, cousin," says Juliet. "The things my father said, the names he called me. . . ." She shakes her head, as though e'en the memory of it pains her. "Look you here." She holds up a small vial.

"What have you?"

"A wedding gift, if thou wilt. From Friar Laurence."

I am now thoroughly perplexed. "Perfume?"

"Nay. Poison."

"*Jules!*"

"'Tis not precisely poison," she qualifies. "Rather, 'tis a miraculous draught, a liquor that shall make me appear dead."

"I know of the stuff. The Healer spoke of it; she brewed a small batch for the Friar, being that they share an interest in herbs and their properties, using a recipe sent to him some years ago by a noblewoman from Denmark."

"Ah," Juliet says. "'Tis imported, then."

"'Tis risky. 'Tis unproven."

"'Tis all I have."

I wrap my arms around her; we sit down on her bed, the vial balanced there betwixt us, and Juliet tells me all that hath transpired, beginning with this morning's brutal quarrel with her lord and lady.

"I was determined to find a way out of this union," she tells me, wringing her hands in her lap. "If my father would not grant me a reprieve, then I vowed I would find my own deliverance . . ." she pauses, lowering her eyes, ". . . upon the point of a dagger."

My heart gives a mighty thump. "Juliet, never say it!"

She meets my gaze again. "And what wouldst thou advise?"

"Anything but that! 'Tis suicide you speak of. A mortal sin!" I take her chin firmly in my hand. "And the most cowardly of acts, be sure of it."

"Is it?" she asks, defiant now. "I hold no other power. My sire decides to whom I shall be married and when. And should I recoil from his choice, he will decide that I am no longer welcome in this home. Were I to lodge a knife in my breast, now, that is no one's choice but my own."

I cannot help myself. I slap her, hard, across her face . . . so hard, my palm stings.

The force of the clout turns Juliet's face away from me. For a moment she is still, her chin upon her shoulder. Then, slowly she lifts her head. Her cheek is stained red from the impact of my hand. Good. I surely hope it smarts.

"Do not await my apology," I tell her. "For 'tis not about to come."

Her voice comes evenly, strangely calm, as though she has not heard me. "I went to the friar's cell to ask his counsel, and 'twas this liquid he gave me. I am to drink it tonight. When the day of my marriage dawns I will be found here under its magical spell. Dead they will call me, and who is to know if my lord and lady will grieve? Mayhap they will be glad to be done with me, disobedient wretch that I am. Of course, my demise shall deprive my father of the superior son for whom he so desperately wishes, and my mother will be near inconsolable o'er the fine food that shall go to waste when the wedding feast is called off. Although I suppose it will just as sufficiently feed the mourners who come to see me buried."

I cannot believe this that I hear. My mouth has fallen open. She goes on.

"The good friar has already sent a Franciscan brother to deliver a missive to Romeo exiled in Mantua. The dispatch tells him to come for me in the tomb, where he shall find me seemingly deceased, but in truth, I shall be on the verge of waking. Hence we shall away, together, to Mantua, to live happily as man and wife."

"Pray, cousin, what will you do if the potion be faulty, if you do not appear dead on the morrow? Wilt thou accept it as fate's decision and get thyself up and to the church to marry a second husband?"

"Never."

Juliet withdraws from beneath her pillow a most lethal-looking blade.

"You may slap me again, if you must," she says in that same flat tone. "But if I be forced to choose betwixt marriage to Paris and true death, I will put my faith in this knife. And in my only power, which is to die at my own hand."

O, she is so very, very young, and so afraid. There is no wonder she has lost all trust. I snatch her weapon away.

"There are other daggers," she whispers.

I scowl at her. "Odd, but just days ago you feared having e'en one blade about your person."

"I have aged a lifetime since then."

"You have aged not at all. You are still every bit a child!"

She rolls her eyes petulantly.

"Shame on thee, Juliet. Shame! What you describe is not power; nay, 'tis the very opposite of power. It is weakness and stupidity and indolence and defeat. Mark me, cousin, there is nothing mighty in quitting life. The only victory is summoning the audacity to stay. If you truly wish to exert power in the face of your father's cruelty, there is only one thing for you to do."

"And what is that?" she asks.

"Live. No daggers, no potions. Live, and tell your lord that you cannot marry for you have already married."

"He will turn me out, I told thee."

"Let him. Romeo will return for you, and rather than spirit you away in secret from a crypt he can collect you at your own front door. You will have naught to fear from old Capulet after that."

Juliet lowers her eyes to the vial. "'Tis easier this way."

"Aye. 'Tis why I so dislike the plan."

And having said so, I take the blade and march from her chamber, slamming the door as I go.

TYBALT

One advantage of this almost-death is that I can be everywhere and see everything.

The disadvantage, of course, is that I can do nothing to influence what I see.

I have remained here, a ghost in Juliet's chamber, since her return from the friar's cell. I heard her tell Rosaline of a strange sleeping poison, I saw her reveal a dagger, and I witnessed the desperate moment in which Rosaline was driven to slap her hard. Relieved was I when Roz claimed Juliet's weapon, but still I was compelled to stay and watch over my beloved, confused young cousin.

"Ah, well," she whispers, as though she feels me here, "there are other daggers. I've one stashed here in the darkest corner of my wardrobe cabinet, beneath my satin undergarment. Rosaline is welcome to the blade she took; I am fortunate the nurse did not detect it when she dug through this soft finery in search of bridal attire. I've hidden yet another blade beneath an ivy-filled urn upon the balcony. Rosaline, you're welcome to the dagger, for the one on the balcony is longer, and this one concealed in the folds of my pale pink chemise be the sharpest of the three. I shall pray awhile before I drink. And then, a toast to my beloved I shall make."

I watch as she uncorks the demon bottle. If the friar is true, tomorrow she shall be borne to the Capulet tomb, where she will stay dead but awhile, then awaken to kiss her husband, Romeo, the ghost of the flavor of this mysterious liquor still present on her lips.

"How shall it taste, I wonder?" she asks aloud.

And so she prays, then drinks her sleeping potion, not knowing if it is to be trusted. Mayhap she believes herself courageous for tempting Providence so boldly, but I see her action is more cowardly than brave. So childish is Juliet that the prospect of having to fight for what her heart desires frightens her enough to provoke a deed so dangerous.

I watch through the night.

And pray myself that the friar's draught keeps its promise.

Daylight comes and with it the girl's nurse. She calls out, but no answer does Juliet make. The nurse draws back the bed curtains and sees the dismal scene. Juliet, her skin gone gray as a winter's sunset, the gown she was to wear at her wedding still hung upon a peg beside the bed.

"Lady, lady, lady!" she cries, and reaches 'neath the cover to find that Juliet's flesh is cold. *"Help, help! My lady's dead!"*

Juliet's mother comes now, and when she sees the pretty corpse, she falls to her knees by her daughter's bed wailing, "O, me, my child, my only life."

And here is my uncle, Juliet's father, coming to collect the bride-to-be but finding instead a pretty corpse. His wife sobs, *"She's dead, she's dead. . . ."*

Capulet's misery comes in a keening howl.

I long for a voice, for with it I would remind the man that 'twas only yesterday he called her baggage and threatened to toss her out of his house.

Well, she will be out of his house now, won't she?

He loved her only when she took commands, and her lady mother was equally unreliable with her affections.

I would damn them both to hell, but as they huddle beside their dead child, I realize they are already there.

ROSALINE

How many living cousins is one girl expected to mourn? And in the course of a single week! For there lies Juliet, believed dead, and all those who grieved so recently for Tybalt have gathered here again to pay their last respects.

I have come with the others to the tomb and bow my head and ask God's blessing, but 'tis fraud, all of it. Mayhap they wonder why I shed no tears. Mayhap they think me in some manner of shock, or denial. O, how I tire of these false funerals for the living.

As we enter the tomb, the nurse corners me beside an urn of withering roses. Her ruddy cheeks are damp with tears.

" 'Twas I who found her, you know."

"Yes, nurse. I know."

Now the cleric begins his ritual:

Part Two

In nomine Patris,

et Filii,

et Spiritus Sancti . . .

The candles are lit, the psalms are sung. The tomb is a shadowy place that smells of long-dead flesh and brittle bones, yet I am pleased that my cousin hath found a way to come here. For when her love collects her, she will leave this place enjoying high spirits. Whereas all others who have come here dead have left here, well, *as* spirits.

'Tis a comical thought. O, I will laugh. I know it, I will laugh at my own musings and clever wordplay, and if I laugh they will not think me shocked, but mad! I feel the giggle bubbling in my throat . . . I clench my teeth against the happy sound . . .

And of a sudden, it occurs to me that after tonight, when Romeo carries his bride off to Mantua, much time will pass ere I am able to see her again. Or perhaps all time. Perhaps they will embrace their exile so thoroughly that they will abscond to someplace e'en farther than Mantua and cut all ties with their quarreling kin.

Juliet, my darling cousin, my dearest friend, will be gone from me.

I shall miss her. I shall miss her deeply.

Good-bye, sweet Juliet. May God keep you well in Mantua.
I pray you'll travel safe and find yourself welcome. And
above all else, I pray that your Romeo will prove
himself worth the trouble.

ROMEO

My man, Balthasar, did bring me news of the end of the world.

O, 'tis not the end of earth, nor sky, nor heaven nor hell—nay, those worlds go on, eternal, unaltered. 'Tis only my world that ends here, now, today.

The beginning of the end of it is Juliet's death; the end of the end shall be my own, and to that end I have coerced a needy apothecary to disregard the edicts of Mantua by selling to me a potion bent for death. He at first denied me, then saw my gold. And so he sold the draught, and having convinced him to defy the law, I have enabled myself to defy the stars.

For if I cannot live with Juliet, I will surely die with her!

No matter the things I shall be missing. I shall not

think on them. I shall not wonder about all the games of billiards and pall-mall I shall miss, or the nights playing hands of basset with my fellows, wagering wisely on the turn of the cards and gladly relieving them of their ducats and silver. I will not think of the untasted sips of well-aged wine, nor of all the dances that will go undanced, the duels unduelled, the books I shall ne'er read nor all the good trouble I will not be round to cause. I suppose I do not care that I will never again best Benvolio in a bocce match. Nay. 'Tis better to die, than to drink wine or play cards or dance or duel or bowl in a world where there is no Juliet.

'Tis the end of Juliet, and in the end, she is the only world that matters.

Balthasar complains that the march from Mantua is a taxing one. I speak not at all, clutching my vial of poison. When we reach the boundary of Verona, I lead him direct to the churchyard.

"Hold, take this letter," I tell him. "Early in the morning see thou deliver it to my lord and father. Upon thy life, I charge thee, whate'er thou hearest or seest, stand all aloof and do not interrupt me in my course."

"I will be gone, sir," Balthasar assures me, "and not trouble you."

As he takes his leave, methinks I hear him whisper that he will hide nearby, but I am too intent upon my purpose to pay him any heed.

TYBALT

I find myself hovering above the cemetery. Earlier this day was Juliet borne to the family tomb and fraudulently laid to rest. I could not bring myself to watch it.

But I am here now. I've come to my family's tomb like a petal upon the wind, blown here without consent. Mayhap the universe knew what I would find.

'Tis Romeo, working a mattock upon the tomb's heavy gate; and in the shadows, Paris. The count believes that Romeo will commit some further misdeed (ha, what worse could be done?) upon the Capulet dead. Bravely, Paris shows himself and apprehends Romeo, whom he thinks to be a villain.

"Good gentle youth," says Romeo, *"tempt not a desp'rate man."* There is a wild calm in his eyes, a bitter serenity that

smacks of danger and madness. *"I beseech thee, put not another sin upon my head by urging me to fury. I come hither arm'd against myself."*

So Romeo means to take his own life here at the mouth of the Capulet tomb! But Paris marks not Romeo's despair. He draws his blade.

Romeo too produces a weapon. The fine steel gleams in the crystalline glow of a hot moon. Paris is worthy, but Romeo is both skillful and hopeless, a deadly blend. The swords collide and echo only once. Paris falls, wounded upon the point of the same sword that made a ghost of me. I can see that Romeo relishes this victory not at all. He hangs his head, dropping his weapon upon the tomb's threshold.

Paris has a single breath remaining and uses it to request a boon of his killer. *"If thou be merciful,"* the count appeals, *"open the tomb, lay me with Juliet."*

Odd it seems to me, but Romeo complies. Mayhap he recognizes the truth of Paris's feelings. Mayhap in his misery he has lost the capacity for spite and jealousy. He brings his rival into the tomb and does deposit him near to Juliet.

It is grim inside. My own body would have lain here these many hours had Rosaline not seen to it that a counterfeit corpse be placed in my stead upon the bier.

When Paris, the unwed groom, is settled dead in the tomb, Romeo makes to Juliet. Would that I could inform him, would that I could make it known that in time she will awaken.

"*Eyes, look your last!*" he cries, his words ringing off the walls of the crypt like handfuls of broken glass. "*Arms, take your last embrace! And, lips . . .*"

Romeo leans o'er Juliet and kisses her cool lips, then uncorks a small bottle and drinks from it. I would dash it from his grasp, but I am only a shimmer; I am air and regret.

"*O, true apothecary!*" invokes Romeo. "*Thy drugs are quick. Thus with a kiss I die.*"

'Tis not long ere Friar Laurence comes; he enters the tomb to first find the bloodied sword. Now he spies he who did wield it—Romeo—and then the victim—Paris— upon whom the wrath was wrought.

"*Romeo,*" cries the friar. "*O, pale! Who else? What, Paris too? And steep'd in blood?*"

I see the fear upon the cleric's countenance, a tightness that looks not unlike guilt.

Suddenly, upon the stony slab Juliet does stir. God, how it distresses me to see the hope in her eyes, the smile of pure confidence she gives to him. She is life itself, and all the happy anticipation and trust it holds. The friar turns to her as she rises.

"*Where is my lord?*" sweet Juliet inquires of her confessor. "*I do remember well where I should be, and there I am. Where is my Romeo?*"

The friar delivers to her the horrific facts. Her eyes fall to where Romeo lies, a true and loyal bridegroom. Her hopeful aura does falter now. Tears like melted diamonds glisten in her eyes.

Now sounds from without frighten the friar, and he beseeches Juliet join him in his escape, but the child resists with an impassioned shake of her head.

"Go, get thee hence," she tells him, *"for I will not away."*

The friar makes a hasty exit, leaving Juliet alone among the dead. How small she looks, and how abandoned. O, if only I could go to her and urge her not to act imprudently. But pain usurps reason, and she reaches toward the vial still clutched in Romeo's hand. She tilts it, but no poison does it yield.

"O, churl, drunk all and left no friendly drop to help me after? I will kiss thy lips, haply some poison yet doth hang on them. Thy lips are warm." Juliet takes her kiss from Romeo, e'en as outside the guards approach. To my great relief, she remains alive.

In one graceful motion she removes Romeo's dagger from its sheath. All that I am wills her not to do it, but all that I am is nothing. Without trepidation, Juliet lifts the weapon.

"This is thy sheath," she whispers to the blade, then plunges it into her breast. *"There rust, and let me die."*

I watch, helpless, as my young cousin drops in a heap upon the chest of her beloved, blood seeping through her gown's bodice like a blooming rose.

Though I expect to see Juliet's ghost rise hand-in-hand with Romeo's to join me in this limbo, no spirits ascend. Death defers. Their dying, like mine own, is delayed. I can feel Juliet's spirit lingering there inside her corporeal self. For a moment, I pray that she will find the strength to heal, to live, but I can see the wound is deep, and already her blood is pooling on the floor. A voice that is the Universe tells me that it is, indeed, her time to die. But this child's soul refuses.

Wordlessly, I call out to her, angel to angel, ghost to ghost. *Surrender, sweet cousin. Let go.*

Her spirit shudders. I sense she is afraid. Her soul regrets what her hand hath done, and the tomb is filled with the force of her self-censure. Shame darkens her spirit; she prays that it all be undone.

But there is nothing for it. 'Tis irreversible. She is angry and ashamed, and because she willingly embraced that blade, she doubts that heaven will have her.

She is wrong, but I am not dead enough to tell her so.

Mayhap she needs a champion. A champion who long ago did teach her to turn cartwheels and encouraged her to climb the tall trees in her father's orchard.

Aye. I shall escort the child. Who better than I, her cousin and friend, to see her safely to eternity?

I waver, flicker, and now I spiral, up and out above the cemetery, drifting like smoke through Verona's sky, toward the place where my body waits.

I return to myself to die.

ROSALINE

I sense the precise moment my cousin dies.

Here in the Healer's cottage, Benvolio looks on from a chair whilst I sit on the floor teaching Viola to inscribe the characters of her name. Of a sudden, a feeling of awesome dread swells up within me.

I spring to my feet and hurry 'cross the room to Tybalt, sprawled before the fire. 'Tis as though, for just a heart-beat's breadth, the magnitude of his spirit surrounds me in an ethereal embrace, in waves of warmth and affection, Tybalt's voice in soundless song comes to mine ear:

Farewell, my precious cousin, and mourn me not, for in your heart I shall outlive myself.

The disappointment is nearly too intense to bear. It

lasts a mere moment, and in its wake there comes a gentle peace, a quiet kind of contentment that is not quite joy, but close. I recognize it to be acceptance. One moment, Tybalt lived, and the next, he ceased to be. Whatever ghostly part of him remained in our midst is now undeniably absent forever from this world.

"He is gone," I tell the Healer.

She presses her finger to his throat and nods.

I turn to Benvolio, who is already on his feet, preparing to assist me in bearing Tybalt's body to the Capulet tomb.

A knock sounds on the door. The Healer opens it to reveal Friar John. A quaking dread erupts in me. This is the brother whom Friar Laurence sent to Mantua to inform Romeo of Juliet's temporary death and that he should come tonight to claim her in the tomb. But if he is here, then clearly, Romeo has not received his instructions.

"Good friar, what happened?"

The elderly brother explains that, indeed, some unlucky confusion did prohibit him from bringing Friar Laurence's message to Romeo earlier.

I grasp the old friar's shoulders. "When is Juliet due to awaken?"

"Friar Laurence calculates that her sleeping potion will wear off within the half hour. Not to worry, for he has already gone to the Capulet tomb. He shall be there when the lady doth awaken."

His reply is made in a voice so rasping that I am compelled to pull over a chair and guide him into it.

"Aye, I must sit," he gasps. "But just for a bit. 'Tis still my task to reach Mantua and beckon Romeo home to claim his bride." He breaks off, in a fit of coughing. He smiles weakly and promises, "All will be well, all will be—" but more coughing cuts him short.

The Healer brings the friar a horn cup of cool water, which he drinks in grateful gulps. I study the old cleric, taking in his drawn face, his gaunt form. If this short jaunt from Friar Laurence's cell to the Healer's cottage has left him weak and breathless, he surely will not make it to Mantua without incident.

Still, Romeo must be told. But, hell's teeth, by whom? I must go to the tomb to whisper the prayers of interment o'er Tybalt's soul, so *I* cannot hie to Mantua. And Benvolio's strength is required to carry Tybalt in stealth to the cemetery.

Now Viola tugs upon my sleeve. As though the child has read my mind, she looks up at me with a most determined expression. "I know the way to Mantua," she says. "I will find Romeo and tell him all."

I shake my head firmly. "No. 'Tis too dangerous for a child to walk alone at night. There may be bandits—"

"I am fast," she assures me. "And small. If I keep to the trees, no thief will e'en notice me." Her pretty face is serious when she adds, "Please, Lady Rosaline."

I turn to Benvolio. He considers a moment, then nods.

"This little one is brave and capable." He grins. "Rather like thee, my love."

I remove a lantern from a hook beside the door and hand it to the child, then kiss her soundly on the top of her head as Benvolio reverently lifts Tybalt into his arms.

"Go ye forth quickly, Rosaline," says Friar John, "and tell Friar Laurence we've enlisted a valiant angel to carry out my part in this plan." He pauses to smile at Viola, tracing the sign of the cross with his thumb upon her brow. "Encumbered as he is, Benvolio will follow you at a slower pace. Viola can walk with him as far as the cemetery and aid his progress with her lantern."

Viola holds the lamp while I light it. Once the flame has sprung to life, she dips a quick curtsy to Friar John. I do the same.

With lifeless Tybalt in Benvolio's arms, we three depart into the night.

Verona sleeps in heat and silence. Once beyond the square, I break away from my companions, hastening toward the graveyard. Behind me, I hear Benvolio and Viola singing soft and sweetly together as they traverse the quiet night. Their voices fade away as I put more distance between us.

Minutes later, I arrive at the churchyard and enter the long passage into the Capulet tomb. The friar is within, but—damnation—he is far from alone. I conceal myself in the shadows of the dim passageway and peer into the crypt. In this way I learn that Viola's brave excursion shall be for naught, as Romeo has already returned to Verona.

He lies dead.

Paris, with the life bled out of him, is also present.

And Juliet, who was expected to awaken from her potion-induced demise, is here as well. She too is dead. She is dead again. And this time, I fear, 'tis real. For there is a knife in her chest. And that, I imagine, would be a difficult thing to fake.

I remain near the tomb's entrance unseen and make a quick accounting of those others present and alive: the prince. Romeo's man, Balthasar. Paris's page (I believe 'twas he who wisely summoned the guards) and several members of the watch, holding spades and bloody weaponry discovered on these holy premises. Juliet's parents, along with Montague, sire to Romeo, who announces that his wife is dead. He blames her demise on grief o'er Romeo's exile and weeps first for his deceased wife, then his dead son.

In the pale light of funeral candles, Friar Laurence tells the tragic tale of the secret wedding, the sleeping potion, the undelivered letter, and Juliet waking to find Romeo dead. He can only guess that, after he'd gone, Juliet could not bear to live without her Romeo and so used her husband's blade to do violence upon herself.

My uncle and aunt, having already accepted their daughter's death once, are twice tortured now to learn she lived but lives no more.

Now Balthasar produces for the prince a letter Romeo had bid him deliver to Montague, and the contents of that missive confirm the friar's report. Paris's page informs all that Paris came only to strew flowers o'er Juliet's death-bed, but Romeo interrupted him and a swift battle ensued.

I have heard enough. My sadness is second only to my frustration o'er the frailty of these many strategies, all of which were contrived to bring about happiness, all of which brought grief instead.

I make to leave in secret, and begin backing toward the passageway. A hand alights upon my shoulder. 'Twould shock me not at all were I to turn and see a ghost, for this place is afire with phantom energies this night. But it is not a spirit, rather a young servant of the prince. He must have been left to wait outside.

"Lady Rosaline," he whispers, "Benvolio sends me from the churchyard to give thee word of his arrival." His voice trembles a soft echo in the musty hall.

"Where does Benvolio hide himself?"

"In the shadow of the tallest gravestone," the boy answers. "There is a woman as well, bearing a satchel. She conceals herself near the trunk of the yew tree."

"I thank thee for bringing me this news."

The boy turns to go, then glances back. "O, and Lady, noble Benvolio doth carry a dead man in his arms."

I nod, showing no surprise, which surprises the boy indeed. "Is there also a comely child with him?"

The boy nods. "Carrying a lamp."

I instruct the lad to explain to Viola that she need not set out for Mantua.

When he has gone, I look once more to the sight inside the crypt. Romeo's father is promising a golden sculpture of fair Juliet, who bleeds before us. Capulet vows to mirror the gesture, by bestowing a statute of his own in the likeness of Romeo, his lost son-in-law. Now the prince speaks a swift and eloquent eulogy, which ends with the names of these spent angels resounding in the flickering gloom of the burial vault:

"For never was a story of more woe, than this of Juliet and her Romeo."

I shiver in the stony tomb and whisper, "Jules," but the word is lost in the noise of grief. Juliet's mother and father shudder in each other's arms, their tears as warm as their newly dead daughter's blood. The prince indicates his desire to go, and the others follow.

I press myself further into the gloom, ducking into a shadowy niche that holds a great crucifix to keep from being seen as the procession passes. Lady Capulet cries, her husband bellows his anguish, and old Montague staggers by, mute with mourning.

When they are gone, I step into the heart of the burial chamber and gaze upon the shared stillness of the newlyweds.

Now Benvolio, carrying Tybalt's body, ducks into the darkness to join me. At the sight of the deceased lovers, his eyes grow misted, but his steady hold does not falter. He cradles the lifeless Tybalt in his arms as though they had been friends. Viola stands at his heel, looking sadly from Romeo to Juliet.

The Healer comes as well, her tools and remedies safe inside her satchel. A beggar brought her news of some commotion in the churchyard only moments after I left her cottage.

The four of us stand in the musty silence, our eyes fixed on the dead lovers. And then . . .

Intuition draws me closer.

There is something wrong, more wrong than just that which appears to be wrong—or is it something right? My soul goes cold, then, as suddenly, it warms. Hope demands I force myself to recognize what eludes me. I lean down and summon all my courage so that I may more closely scrutinize these pretty corpses.

And . . .

Yes!

Hope has not mocked me! For Juliet's fingers round the dagger's handle are not yet gnarled with death's rigor, and Romeo's lips are a ways from blue enough.

Instinct guides me. Trembling, I place my fingertips to Juliet's throat. I sense only a whisper of a pulse, but mayhap it will be enough.

Now, Romeo . . .

I touch his wrist. 'Tis clammy, cold, but he too lives.

O, God save the apothecary whose poison is so poor!
And now do I recall the words I felt when Tybalt died:
Mourn me not, for in your heart I shall outlive myself.

And whispered in harmony with those are the pro-
phetic words I myself did speak to Juliet on the night of
Capulet's feast.

A change of heart, I'd said then. I repeat it now, aloud. "A
change of heart . . ."

The phrase seems to tremble on the air. I turn to the
Healer—she knows what I am thinking.

A girl can pray for a miracle. Or she can perform one.

"You think to replace Juliet's ruined heart with Tybalt's
healthy one," the Healer says evenly, but her eyes are dark
with trepidation.

"I do."

Benvolio consigns Tybalt's body to the nearest bier so
that he can place his hands upon my shoulders. "Rosaline, you play God in such an act," he says softly.

"Mayhap, but then 'twas God who gave me these steady
hands, this worthy mind."

"I fear Tybalt has been dead too long, and Juliet has
already lost a great amount of blood," the Healer warns.
"'Tis an immeasurable risk."

"What greater risk is there than doing nothing?" I
demand, my voice low and laced with frenzy.

"We can remove the dagger," the healer says sensibly.
"And stitch the wound. Perhaps—"

"She has punched a hole in her heart!" I cry, sensing hysteria bearing down on me. "Such a thing cannot be mended with mere knotted string! Tybalt's heart is our only hope." In one swift motion, I reach for the knife in Juliet's chest and pull it free. A thick spray of blood spatters my face in crimson droplets, which I ignore. I begin to pace round the tomb in long, fast strides, propelled by the force of the need I have to heal.

"Here is what I will do. First I will crack Juliet's breastbone in twain! Benvolio, I will require your assistance in this, as I am not strong enough to do it alone. I shall slice into her skin and open her chest cavity. She will bleed profusely, but if I can cinch the most prolific artery . . ." I pause, scanning the dank room. "With what? What might I use to fashion a clamp. . . ." My gaze falls on the ring Romeo wears, the very one Juliet herself did bestow on him. "Aye, this ring will do for a clamp."

"Rosaline, no——" Benvolio comes over to wrap his arms around me, but I jerk free and continue to stamp across the stony floor.

"Of course, we must also open Tybalt. Healer, you will have to reach inside to massage the organ, I think, while it is still attached. Yes." I close my eyes and imagine. The surgery unfolds in my mind's eye—I am watching myself save Juliet.

"I will sever Juliet's heart from the tangle of veins and vessels that feed it. 'Twill be slick, I think, slippery, but I will mind my grip and cut cautiously so as not to damage any other organs." I open my eyes and turn to Benvolio. He only gapes at me, his skin has gone ashen.

I hold up Romeo's dagger, stained with his wife's warm blood, and examine it. " 'Tis sharp and sufficiently pointy," I observe. "Mean enough to kill her. Therefore, it will surely be sweet enough to save her."

"Child," the Healer appeals. "Please. Hear thyself. 'Tis madness you speak."

"Madness?" I shout. "O speak not to me of madness! Madness would be allowing these two beautiful, impetuous . . . *idiots* . . . to die without attempting to make things right." I raise my arms and shout to the low ceiling so that my words fall back on me like fiery meteors. "I must do something. I must heal them!"

Frantic, hopeful, terrified, and confident, I whirl around so that I am standing above Juliet's dying body with the knife poised, preparing to plunge it into her chest.

BENVOLIO

I do not know for sure how long Rosaline stood with Romeo's knife poised above Juliet's chest. But in the end, she made no cut. She broke no bone. She simply placed the dagger carefully alongside her cousin's body and knelt beside the bier, in the bloody puddle on the floor.

And now I recognize that, along with the odor of bodies long dead, the airless tomb reeks also of fresh blood. A sound comes from my belly, then from my throat.

O, I will not swoon. Nay, I will not faint. I will not . . .

. . . O, 'tis no use.

Last I recall is Rosaline looking at me o'er her shoulder—does she smile? Aye, she does, just a bit, a smile filled with heartache, and then . . .

Darkness.

ROSALINE

The Healer likely assumes that I have chosen not to gift Juliet with Tybalt's heart for reasons that are medical in nature. I would wager she thinks that my good sense has triumphed and that I lowered the knife in deference to divine Providence and my own inexperience. But this is not so. Here is why I stayed my hand:

For e'en if my brave procedure did somehow keep my beloved cousin alive, I was not sure that Juliet would be capable of loving Romeo with Tybalt's heart.

And Romeo, I am certain, will live. I rise from the floor, feeling the heaviness of my blood-soaked skirt as I move toward Romeo, bidding the Healer to bring me her satchel.

From within it I choose a small flask in which there is a thick syrup. 'Tis a precious but unpalatable concoction derived from the *ipecacuanha* shrub; the plant is unknown in Italy, and this small quantity is all that remains of some given to the Healer by a stranger who traveled here from a place he called Brazil.

I take hold of Romeo's chin and force his mouth open to pour a stream of the syrup onto his tongue, then I tilt his head farther backward. When I am satisfied that the liquid has reached his stomach, I quickly shift him to his side, careful to aim him away from the place on the floor where Benvolio has landed.

The syrup is effective. In moments, Romeo begins to gag, then heave, then vomit violently, purging his system of the poison he's ingested. I apply pressure to his forehead as he upchucks and try to ignore the unpleasant smells and sounds that emanate from him.

When at last Romeo has finished emptying his guts onto the floor I use a clean rag to wipe his mouth. He breathes normally now, and the blue tint has vanished from his lips.

I turn my attention to Benvolio, who is just now coming awake.

"Rosaline?"

"Aye, Benvolio, I am here." I extend my hand to him as he rises unsteadily. "Watch thy step," I caution. "There is blood and vomit everywhere."

"Ah, such a sweet talker is my lady," Benvolio says, an attempt at levity which, surprisingly, I much appreciate. Viola draws near to me and takes my hand. She nods her chin in Juliet's direction.

"She is dead?"

"Dying," I say. "But not dead yet."

Romeo stirs, letting out a ragged groan.

"He is well?" Benvolio asks anxiously.

I then lean close to Romeo's face. "Romeo? Romeo, dost thou hear me?"

Another groan, and then his eyes open. For a moment, he simply stares, then, with a jolt, he sits upright, flinging his arms around me.

"Rosaline! My darling."

Benvolio frowns. *"Darling?"*

I squirm fervently in Romeo's grasp, but he will not release me.

"Rosaline, o, angelic one, I had the most peculiar dream—"

He begins to press urgent kisses onto my neck.

With a grunt, Benvolio takes hold of Romeo's collar and gives a mighty tug.

"Collect thy wits," Benvolio advises. "Then see if thou canst remember who thou shouldst be calling darling."

Romeo's face is blank.

"Think hard, Romeo," Benvolio counsels. "The feast . . . the girl . . . the balcony."

Romeo's eyes widen. "Juliet! O, my Juliet. Then 'twas

not a dream? The wedding? The murders? My exile? The poison?"

Romeo's skin turns pale. "Juliet. My lady wife, my love . . . I found her here, dead—"

"Not dead," I say softly. "She merely appeared thus."

"Then she is alive!"

"For the moment," I reply softly.

"'Tis a most complicated tale," Benvolio offers. "I shall tell thee all, but let us first away from this rank place—"

"No!"

I start at the fierceness of Romeo's refusal.

Benvolio looks to me; I nod. Wordlessly, he takes Viola's hand and leads her out of the tomb while the Healer gathers her paraphernalia. She too makes a silent exit.

I return to where Juliet lies upon the bier and kneel again beside her, leaning to rest my head upon the cool stones of the crypt.

Romeo's hand comes to rest in a brotherly way upon my shoulder as he sits upon a nearby coffin to join me in keeping this solemn vigil.

BENVOLIO

By the blood of Saint Peter, this hath been the longest night of my life.

I sit in the grass of the churchyard waiting for Rosaline and Romeo to emerge from the crypt. I lean against the trunk of the yew and watch Viola with the lantern. She has been teaching herself to read by using the epitaphs upon the tombstones as her primer. The sounds of a summer night fill the cemetery. The darkness is like a ghost; the heat is everywhere.

Rosaline mourns in the tomb, and when she comes out, I shall be here.

ROSALINE

Odd, but one grows used to the stench. And the near-atrophy of one's own muscles becomes a bitter kind of comfort. I have not moved for hours. I look upon Juliet, and tears sting my weary eyes, dampen my cheeks.

"Cry you for her?" comes Romeo's voice o'er my shoulder. "Or for thyself?"

My reply is a small shrug.

"Tell me something, Rosaline," he beseeches, tears welling up in his eyes. "Tell me something of her, this Juliet."

"Your wife," I remind him softly.

"My wife." He drags one hand down his face in frustration. "And yet . . . and yet, I knew her not at all. O, but I loved her so and shall love her forever."

"Never say it!"

My tone brings him up short and he stares at me.

"Never say it," I repeat. The sound is thunderous in the quiet crypt. "Damned fool, how darest thou speak of love?"

I spring up from my knees with unexpected strength to glower down at him and sputter, "*You!* You, Romeo, who loves only with your eyes." I narrow my gaze, letting it slide boldly and meaningfully downward to his midsection. "And with certain other parts of your anatomy."

To his credit, the boy does flush. Still, I am not appeased.

"Love?" I roar, fists clenched. "Bloody hell, that word should leave a blister on thy tongue. Your recklessness, yours and Juliet's, was an affront to true devotion, your irreverence dishonored love. You met and admired one another and impiously called it love. 'Twas quick and bright and dangerous and magical. But you did not *think*. You settled for desire, but did not allow time for love."

"And now," he concedes, "she lies here, dead, as would I, were it not for you."

My bluster subsides, exhausted as I am. More silence falls between us.

"What would you know of her?" I ask.

He ponders a moment. "Her favorite flower to start."

"Roses."

He smiles sadly. "I'd heard her speak of them once. How, by any other name they'd smell as sweet."

"And the girl could surely sit a horse," I add. "Tybalt taught her to ride, e'en to jump. Her command of the Gallic language was legendary, but her mastery of Greek was poor." With a laugh that is part sob, I add, "She liked figs."

"I like figs," says Romeo, and there is something both consoled and tortured in his tone.

Again, we wait a wordless while. The quiet stretches into minutes. Dust spirals in the stale air.

"I could not save her." I do not realize I have spoken the words aloud until I hear them ringing a soft echo in the stony tomb. "I could not revive Tybalt when he fell, I could not unstab Mercutio, and though I nearly tempted Satan by trying, I could not make Juliet whole again with a borrowed heart. For all my wit and wisdom, all my study and sacrifice, I could not and will ne'er be able to undo death."

"You undid my death," he reminds me.

"You were not dead."

"Nor is Juliet."

"Nay, she is worse than dead. She is dying. Dying every moment she lives." I drop my head into my hands and weep softly.

"Why do you suppose she hangs on?" he asks.

"I cannot say," I answer honestly.

He studies her face, his tears falling unabashedly now. "Sweet spouse and stranger," he says, touching her gaunt face, "I daresay I would have truly loved you, if only we had had time to learn what love could be. But then, who is to know if you would have loved me in return? Friar Laurence did admonish us, 'Wisely and slow, they stumble that run fast.'"

Now Romeo slips nimbly from the coffin to his knees and bows his head. I watch as one silken lock of his hair brushes gently across her cheek.

Sweet, so sweet, if only she could feel.

I expect to hear him offer up some prayer that she return to us. Some request to the Almighty Father that they be given a second chance. I expect him to implore our Lord to bring her back, to restore her life.

Instead, I hear him whisper this: "I'm sorry."

I'm sorry.

No more, but enough. 'Tis but one child's apology to another for a hurt which both are too naive to name.

The words fill the shadowy tomb and settle in my heart. *I'm sorry.*

Perhaps I say them aloud, or mayhap I only think them. *I'm sorry, Juliet. Romeo is sorry, and I am sorry. The world and the stars and angels in heaven are sorry.*

I kneel down beside Romeo, tears—his and mine— flowing afresh.

And here is how I know that Juliet sees fit to forgive us: She dies.

Romeo and I step from the tomb to find Benvolio asleep beneath the yew tree. Dawn is breaking softly. Viola is curled kittenlike near his feet.

As I watch these two who are both so precious to me, a cool breeze comes up and trembles upon my face. As I take a moment to savor it, an idea seems to form itself, take shape from somewhere within the nothingness of the zephyr itself.

I explain my plan to Romeo and give him a small part in its execution, which is to awaken Benvolio and bid him collect Viola's brother and grandfather, and bring them with Viola to my mother's house. Romeo agrees to relay the request to Benvolio. I thank him with a hug. "Where wilt thou go after?" I ask.

"To Mantua," he answers easily. "I am dead here in Verona, and it seems that has done this city good. I shall find a life for myself away from here." He presses a chaste kiss to my forehead. "Remember me fondly," he whispers.

"I shall," I say, and mean it.

With that, I hurry away across the churchyard and into the quiet streets toward home.

My uncle Capulet is quite surprised to see me in his hall so early. Viola stands beside me, utterly trusting, though she has no idea why I have brought her to this rich man's home at sunrise. Sebastian is present, hanging back near the door, holding his grandfather's hand. Benvolio too is present.

Tugging his richly embroidered satin dressing gown round his portly middle, my uncle lumbers down the stairs and into the great hall.

"Rosaline! What madness is this that makes you—"
He just now spies Benvolio behind me. "God's blood, be that a Montague in this house?"

"The feud is over, uncle," I remind him tartly. "Or hast thou already forgotten the golden statues?"

He sputters a moment. "Aye," he says at last. "You are welcome here, sir." He nods to Benvolio. I can see it costs him much and feel a flutter of pride for him.

My uncle looks at me with a pompous lift of his chin, to indicate that he has, indeed, proven himself greatly changed. Then he spots the children. I watch his eyes fall to Viola. And I see precisely what I expected—leastways hoped—I would.

For a moment, he cannot summon words, and I know this is because Viola, with her shimmering tangle of dark tresses and shining eyes, looks so verily like Juliet did as a small girl.

"Who be these ragged waifs?" asks my uncle, in a booming tone that cannot conceal the catch in his voice.

Before I can answer, the door behind Benvolio swings open, and Romeo's widowed lord enters, led by Benvolio's own father.

"Montague?" cries my uncle in disbelief. "Feud or no feud, I can conceive of no reason that would bring you to my home at such an hour!"

Old Montague replies by turning up his palms. "Nor can I, but I have been dragged hence by my cousin here."

He motions to Benvolio's father. "He wouldst not tell me wherefore—"

Montague cuts his thought short, his gaze alighting upon Sebastian. Unable to stop himself, he reaches out to roughly ruffle Sebastian's silky hair. The boy favors him with a wide grin, which causes Montague's lower lip to quake. "Such a fine young man," he murmurs.

Now Lady Capulet hastens into the great space. She first takes in the unwarranted spectacle of three Montagues 'neath her roof. Upon seeing Viola and Sebastian, her slender hand does fly to her mouth, but not in time to stifle the cry that comes up in her throat. The noise resonates with the sound of deepest loss—joy and grief, fused in one audible note. Her face flickers a thousand different emotions before she sinks to her knees upon the mirrorlike marble of the floor and opens her arms to the small strangers. Without hesitation, the twins run to her and all but dive into the circle of her motherly embrace.

For just a piece of a second, I allow myself to think of Juliet, so pale and still upon the bier, and then of Romeo, making his solitary way to Mantua.

"These children are orphans," I explain. "They are destitute."

I see Montague pass a glance o'er the twins; his eyes are soft with compassion.

"Henceforth, they and their grandfather shall reside

in the home of Benvolio's father. Benvolio is to become their guardian."

My uncle nods his approval. "A sound plan."

"But what has it to do with us?" my aunt inquires. She holds the children close to her as though she might n'er let them go.

I allow my eyes to meet hers, then my uncle's, then Montague's.

"You three," I pronounce, "shall be their benefactors. You will provide for them. Food, clothing, education— whatever Benvolio deems necessary to their proper upbringing."

The room goes silent.

"Do you understand," I ask of Lord and Lady Capulet and Montague, "what I am giving you?"

My uncle mops his eyes with the back of his hand and nods. His lady smiles up at me o'er the heads of Viola and Sebastian.

'Tis Montague who speaks an answer for them all.

"A second chance," he whispers.

ROSALINE

Benvolio is off to settle the boarders into their new home, a roomy suite in his father's *casa*.

Walking home through the empty streets of Verona, I am glad to be alone. I could not bear to face Benvolio now. My heart aches, and I am sick with the sense of failure. My inexperience is to blame for Juliet's death. Had I known more, I might have saved her.

When I return home, my mother is relieved to see me, and I fall into her arms, wanting desperately to be a child again. I lower myself to a damask-covered divan. My mother sits beside me and listens as I explain all that has happened since we were last together at Juliet's funeral.

"Benvolio loves me," I say, "and I love him too. 'Tis one of the reasons I am leaving."

"Leaving?"

"Mother . . ." my voice is thick. "Mother, what do you think of me?"

Her eyebrows arc upward slightly, and she smiles. "'Tis an odd question."

"I would very much like to know."

My mother draws a deep breath. "I think you are . . . unusual. Aye, thou art most unique, daughter."

They are but kind ways of saying "strange."

"I am sorry," I whisper.

"Whatever for?"

I swipe at a tear that trembles in the corner of my eye. "It cannot be easy to raise a . . . unique . . . child."

"O, it is not easy to raise any sort of child. But I can tell you that bringing up one with a talent and intelligence such as yours has been truly—"

"Difficult?"

"Quite."

"Exhausting?"

"Mmm, yes."

"And frustrating?"

"To be sure."

"Embarrassing?"

"Never!"

"Never?"

My lady smiles and brushes a wisp of hair from my forehead. "Rosaline, my sweet. Don't you know?"

I search her eyes for the answer. "Know what?"

"That you are a miracle! A miracle of grace and goodness. Aye, you are a difficult, frustrating joy of a daughter. As brave and as bright as thou art beautiful. That God saw fit to give you to me is the thing for which I am most grateful in this world."

I swallow hard. "Father . . . he did not feel the same way, apparently."

"We were very young." Her eyes go soft, and there is forgiveness in her voice.

We stare into the fire, sharing the silence.

"Every corner of this city echoes with our recent losses," I say quietly. "I will depart in the morning. For Padua, where I shall devote myself entirely to my studies. 'Twill not erase the bitter failure of Juliet's death. But mayhap by returning to my resolute path, I shall arm myself against failing again."

"How canst thou call thy courage failure?"

"Juliet lives no more." I keep my gaze stern, steady, and address the flames. "What better definition of failure could there be? I have broken my own rules, lady, and now I find I cannot bear to be where Benvolio is. The feud has ceased, aye, but who is to say a new one won't ignite? How can I know that Benvolio will not one day be injured in a fight, impaled by some malcontent's sword? Or, e'en if peace reigns eternal, how do I know he will not be consumed by fever or trampled by a startled stallion or struck by lightning or drowned or choked or burned . . . ?"

"Fie!" My mother frowns. "You are too smart to speak so."

"I am not smart enough. I am in love. And all love comes to heartache in the end."

With that, I curl up on the small couch and sob until I fall asleep.

I awaken in the late afternoon, when a knock sounds from the entry. I hear my mother's maid hurrying to answer the door. Sitting up, I recognize Benvolio's voice greeting the servant.

Sadness wells up in me, laced with regret.

"Send him away," I mutter, but 'tis too late. The servant is showing him into the salon and bows herself out of the room.

"Good morrow, beloved. I've a surprise for thee."

Now there comes a noisy commotion from the entry hall. "What in heaven's name?"

I turn to see Benvolio's father lingering near the door. He seems to be concealing something ungainly behind him, and he is smiling like a little boy!

"Come here!" Benvolio commands in a firm voice.

"Benvolio!" I chide, in spite of my grief. "Do not speak to your father in such a manner."

"I was not speaking to my father. His tone softens when he repeats, "Come here.""

There is the clicking noise of dulled claws on marble tiles. The heaviness in my heart lifts, and I cry out, "Crab!"

At the sound of his name, the dog appears from behind Benvolio's lord, scampers across the entry hall, and bounds into the salon. In the next second, the mutt has leapt onto the divan and is lolling in my lap.

"Hello! Hello, you beautiful dog, you!"

Benvolio reaches down to scratch Crab's ears. "Seems being a hero agrees with the pooch."

Crab barks his agreement.

Out of the corner of my eye, I notice Benvolio's father quietly taking his leave. Benvolio strokes his thumb gently across my cheek, then nudges Crab away so that he may sit beside me on the divan. He kisses me softly, then again, and I accept the warmth of his lips greedily.

After some time, he leans away and studies me, tracing my chin, touching my hair.

"Dost thou know how proud you make me, Rosaline?"

I can only manage a whisper. "Thank you."

"And 'tis not just your incomparable beauty," he amends quickly. "'Tis your sweetness, your unselfish desire to give to those who are in need. And of course, there is that boundless intelligence of yours."

Benvolio hesitates, then goes down on one knee. Ribbons of sunlight shimmer in his hair.

"Now, then," he says, with a small, silky smile, "as I find I am too impatient to await the moonlight, I suppose the glow of sunset will do just as nicely. We have just enjoyed a wealth of kisses, and here I find myself on bended knee . . ."

My eyes go wide as I recall his words the morning we awoke in the grove.

"All that is missing, it seems, is the unusually large gemstone I spoke of, but hold, what have we here?"

From a pocket sewn into the lining of his tunic, he withdraws a small, glistening thing. "Well, what dost thou know." His smile broadens. "I just happen to be in possession of such a jewel after all." He lifts it into a pale streamer of sunlight, and I see that it is a ring, and it does indeed contain a diamond of uncommonly grand proportions.

I can only gape at it.

"Marry me, Rosaline," he says in a trembling whisper. "Marry me."

My heart swells, my knees quiver.

My answer is a single word.

ROSALINE

My escort from Verona is none other than Petru-chio. His ribs have long since healed, and he has not a scar on his handsome face. His man, Grumio, attends us on the journey. As we traverse eastward, the two men torment one another with a friendly fire of jokes and insults. Their comic banter soothes me some and helps to alleviate the despair I carry with me to Padua.

I sought him out, Trooch, having heard that he was leaving Verona to see the world and seek his fortune, which is to say, to find a wife. A rich one.

I on the other hand desire knowledge, and there is nowhere better than Padua, the Università degli Studi di Padova. I am hopeful that, although I am a woman, they will allow me to study there. I have heard tell that this fine university (guided, perhaps, by the light of Renaissance thinking) does not look unfavorably upon intelligent females.

It is a week before we arrive in Padua, dusty and tired, and we go direct to the home of Trooch's friend Hortensio. Before the servant Grumio e'en knocks upon the door, I curtsy to Petruchio.

"My lord, I thank thee for thy guardianship on this excursion. I shall leave thee to thy task now and set off to see to mine own."

"You are most humbly welcome, Rosaline," Trooch replies. He bows gallantly, then catches me in a hug. "Pretty child, I shall pray to the saints to guide you in your worthy pursuits. Study well, learn much, and I suggest you pay particular attention to the science of healing injured hearts, for lovely as you are, you will surely break your share of them here in Padua."

His remark is merely innocent flattery, but I cannot help thinking of Juliet.

Grumio produces a crudely drawn map from his satchel—directions to the university. "'Tis not far, my lady," he assures me.

"Thank you, Grumio, and good-bye."

I turn to Petruchio and kiss his cheek. "Farewell, friend. I shall listen for news of a wedding. I hope thou findest thyself a lady who is—"

"Wealthy? Beauteous?"

"Smart!"

Trooch laughs.

I round the corner and pause to draw a steadying breath. Not far from here is the university, alive with the greatest, most gifted artists of our day. The University of Padua, with its Palazzo Bo and the Anatomy Theater, where miraculous operations called autopsies are performed for the purpose of academic advancement and scientific understanding.

Not far from here, I shall begin my future. Answer my calling.

Find my dream.

BENVOLIO

I wonder, is she warm enough? Does she sleep sufficient hours, or does she stay awake long into the night, studying scientific texts?

Before she left, I asked Rosaline to be my wife, but she denied me.

I understood. The tragedy was too fresh, the pain too deep when I knelt before her and professed my love.

They say timing is everything.

I am told, in letters from Petruchio, that my love does well in Padua. She is admired by her fellow scholars and has duly impressed the preeminent professors there. I am not surprised.

She has not written me herself. That does not surprise me either. I fear, in her desire to serve the greater good, she has forced herself to forget me. Petruchio informs me in his communiqués that my Rosaline has befriended his own lady love—Katherina, whom he candidly confesses can be something of a shrew. No matter. He adores her, and she him. I am glad for my old friend, but for myself, I suffer quietly.

Rosaline! Such an amazing girl! Nay, woman! O, I do ache for the loss of her, and not a day goes by that I do not send up a prayer for her return. In the meantime, I am busy caring for the twins. Sebastian's cough is long gone, and Viola is being taught to dance, though she prefers books. She often reads to her grandfather and my lord before the fire while Crab lolls nearby, protecting us all.

The golden statues of Romeo and Juliet—impetuous lovers, young strangers—are newly completed and stand now at the center of the city. I pass by them often, though I try not to loiter in their shadows, which fall like grim memories as the sun sets upon Verona.

Mercutio is never far from my thoughts.

And Rosaline is always close within my heart.

ROSALINE

It is the year of our Lord 1599, autumn.

My years in Padua have been well spent. I have not been formally graduated. I fear 'twill be decades before the university, enlightened as it is, will have the courage to bestow a degree upon a lady. But I am well taught and confident. And I am at peace in my soul.

I arrive in Verona in the late afternoon. So different it is from the city I knew. Montagues and Capulets walk in pairs, conversing politely. No one insults his neighbor, and no angry flash of steel catches the last light of the soft, setting sun.

A crimson leaf, the first of autumn, floats by on a cool breeze. My thoughts turn backward briefly to Mercutio, and I understand for the first time that he, more than any of us, would have cherished this peace.

Two households, both alike in dignity in fair Verona . . .

Four years away have made me nostalgic for the place. I meander in the square although the day's commerce has long since ceased. The Healer's cottage stands unchanged. I shall visit her tomorrow, for there is much I want to share with her. At last I shall be able to repay her for all the things she taught me, by teaching her in return.

My mother is away, staying with friends in Venice. In her last letter, she did hint that she had met a most charming gentleman. Mayhap they will marry. I should like that.

I come now to the golden statues of Romeo and Juliet. God's truth, seeing them angers me—better they were alive than fashioned of gold. I look upon them only long enough to note that the nose on Juliet's statue is a bit too narrow, and Romeo's chin, though golden, is not nearly as handsome as was the real thing. 'Tis a mediocre effort, I conclude. Sighing, I walk on.

As twilight comes, I make my way to Benvolio's house. I find him in his father's garden. He stands in profile, admiring a prolific grapevine that swags o'er the wooden arbor.

How beautiful he is, how manly now, e'en more so than when I took my leave of him four years past. The strength I remember is unaltered, the fine structure of his face and the broadness of his shoulders (which I did look upon in my memory every day of my absence) remain. My heart swells.

He does not notice me until Crab, the darling, begins to bark. Benvolio turns.

"I am home," I say foolishly, but it is all I can think of. His eyes are distracting me. I reach down to scratch the dog's ears but cannot remove my gaze from Benvolio. He smiles now. O, but it is the sweetest thing I've ever witnessed, and so sincere. He lifts his hand and gives me a small wave, as though I had departed only days before.

I take one dainty step and then I run, at full speed, to be collected into his arms. He crushes me to him, and I do not mind it a bit.

"I am home," I say again.

"Aye," he agrees softly.

As darkness falls, the rippling peals of church bells from the tower of Saint Peter's seem to welcome the first stars to the sky. Glistening constellations. Stars, aligned at long last, and perfect in the heavens.

Stars to light our way.